RECON ACADEMY

THE HIDDEN FACE OF FREN-Z

FILE NO.
H427678

BY CHRIS EVERHEART
ILLUSTRATED BY ARCANA STUDIO

STONE ARCH BOOKS
MINNEAPOLIS   SAN DIEGO

Recon Academy is published by Stone Arch Books
151 Good Counsel Drive, P.O. Box 669
Mankato, Minnesota 56002
www.stonearchbooks.com

Library of Congress Cataloging-in-Publication Data
Everheart, Chris.
    The Hidden Face of Fren-Z / by Chris Everheart; illustrated by Arcana
Studio.
    p. cm. — (Recon Academy)
    ISBN 978-1-4342-1165-1 (library binding)
    ISBN 978-1-4342-1380-8 (pbk.)
    1. Graphic novels. [1. Graphic novels. 2. Terrorism—Fiction.] I. Arcana
Studio. II. Title.
PZ7.7.E94Hid 2009
[Fic]—dc22   2008032073

Summary: When someone hacks the Federal Reserve Bank computer,
the Recon Academy needs to act fast. If they don't stop the techno thief
soon, the world's economy could crumble. But not even Ryker, the group's
computer whiz, can do it alone. He'll need help from the entire team to
bust this e-bandit and discover the hidden face of Fren-Z.

Designer: Bob Lentz
Series Editor: Donnie Lemke
Series Concept: Michael Dahl, Brann Garvey, Heather Kindseth,
    Donnie Lemke

1 2 3 4 5 6 14 13 12 11 10 09

Printed in the United States of America

〉TABLE OF CONTENTS

〉〉〉〉
ENTER

ライカー

RYKER /COMPUTERS

Born into a world of rising threat —

— they witnessed terror strike the safety of their town.

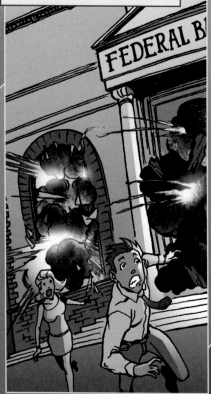

As they grew up, each member developed a unique ability . . .

FORENSICS

MARTIAL ARTS

COMPUTERS

GADGETRY

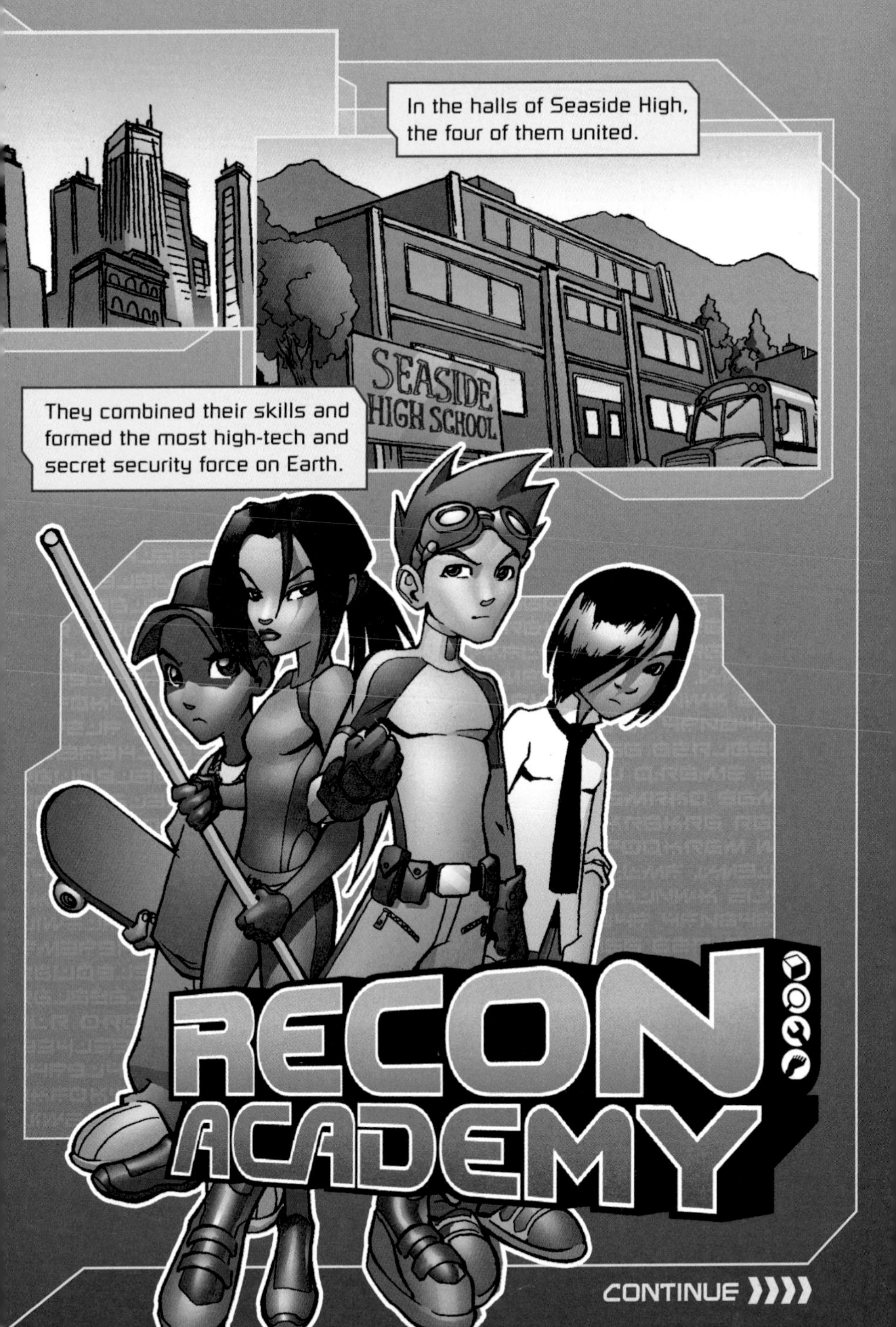

In the halls of Seaside High, the four of them united.
SEASIDE HIGH SCHOOL
They combined their skills and formed the most high-tech and secret security force on Earth.
RECON ACADEMY
CONTINUE

SECTION

FILE NO.: 1437578

1

ACCESS GRANTED)))>

RYKER
COMPUTERS

128718
293829
9283
98289
89
1
109201
192091
1992

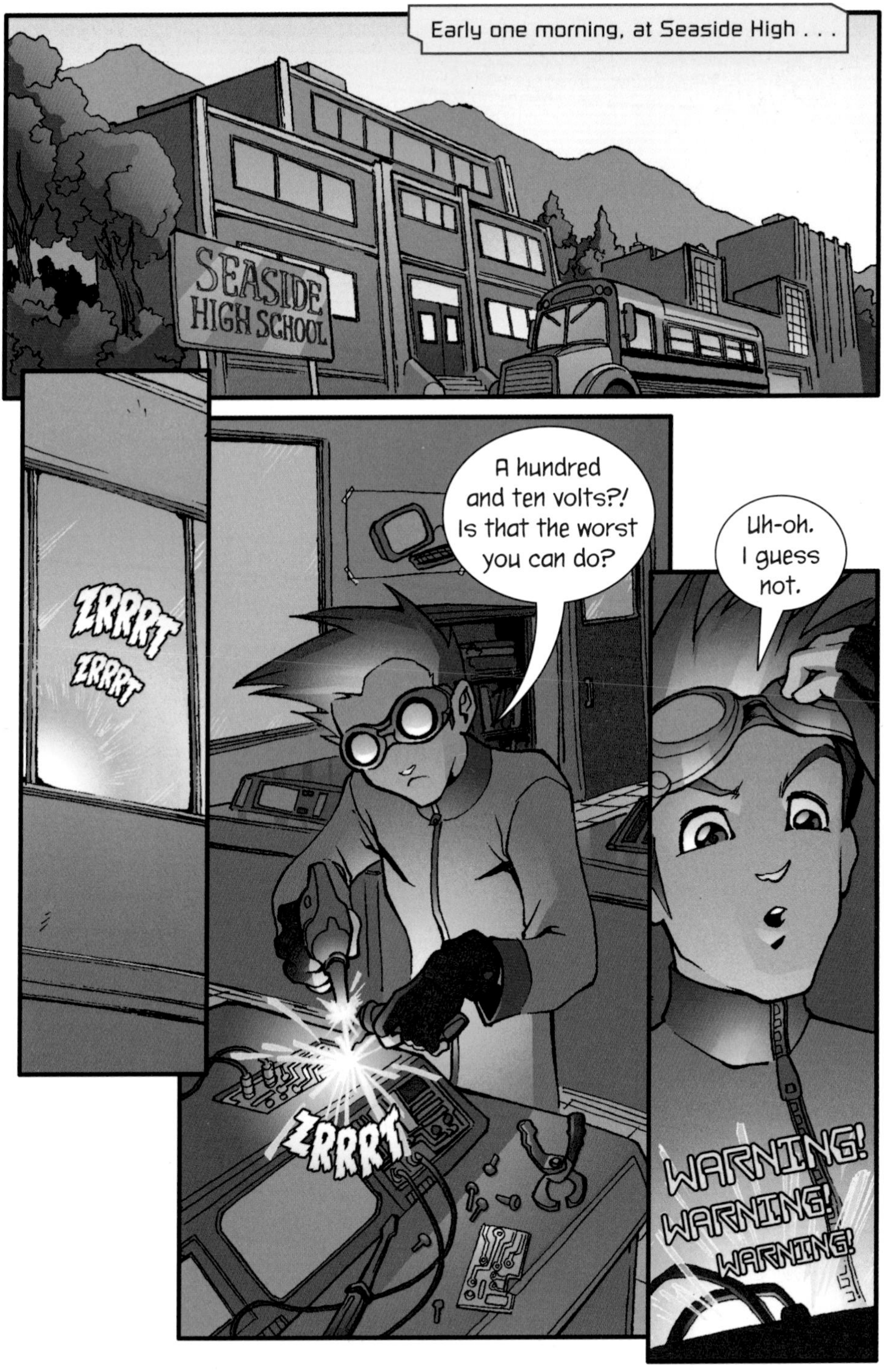
Early one morning, at Seaside High . . .
SEASIDE HIGH SCHOOL
ZRRRT
ZRRRT
A hundred and ten volts?! Is that the worst you can do?
ZRRRT
Uh-oh. I guess not.
WARNING!
WARNING!
WARNING!

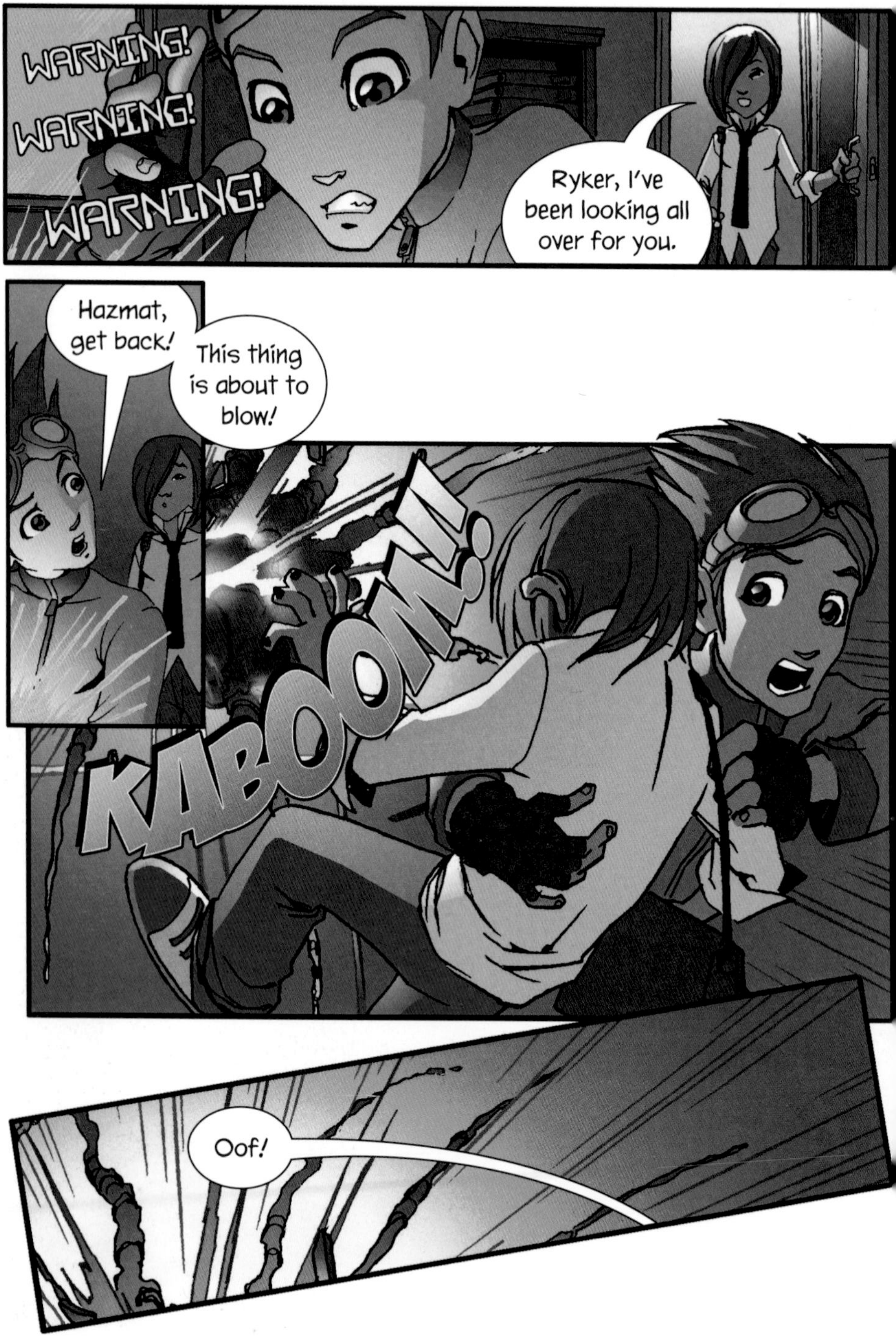
WARNING!
WARNING!
WARNING!
Ryker, I've been looking all over for you.
Hazmat, get back!
This thing is about to blow!
KABOOM!!
Oof!

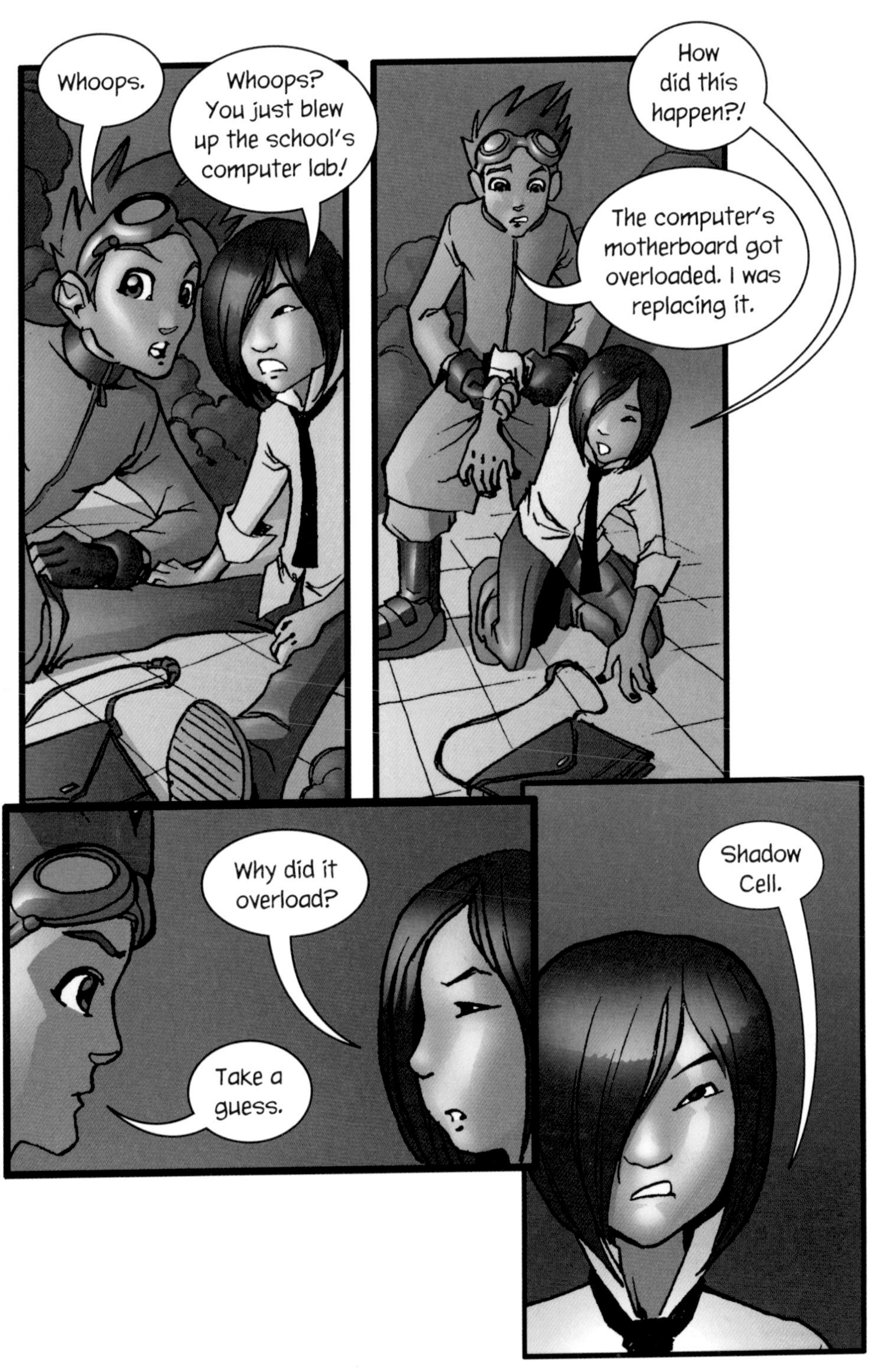
Whoops.
Whoops? You just blew up the school's computer lab!
How did this happen?!
The computer's motherboard got overloaded. I was replacing it.
Why did it overload?
Take a guess.
Shadow Cell.

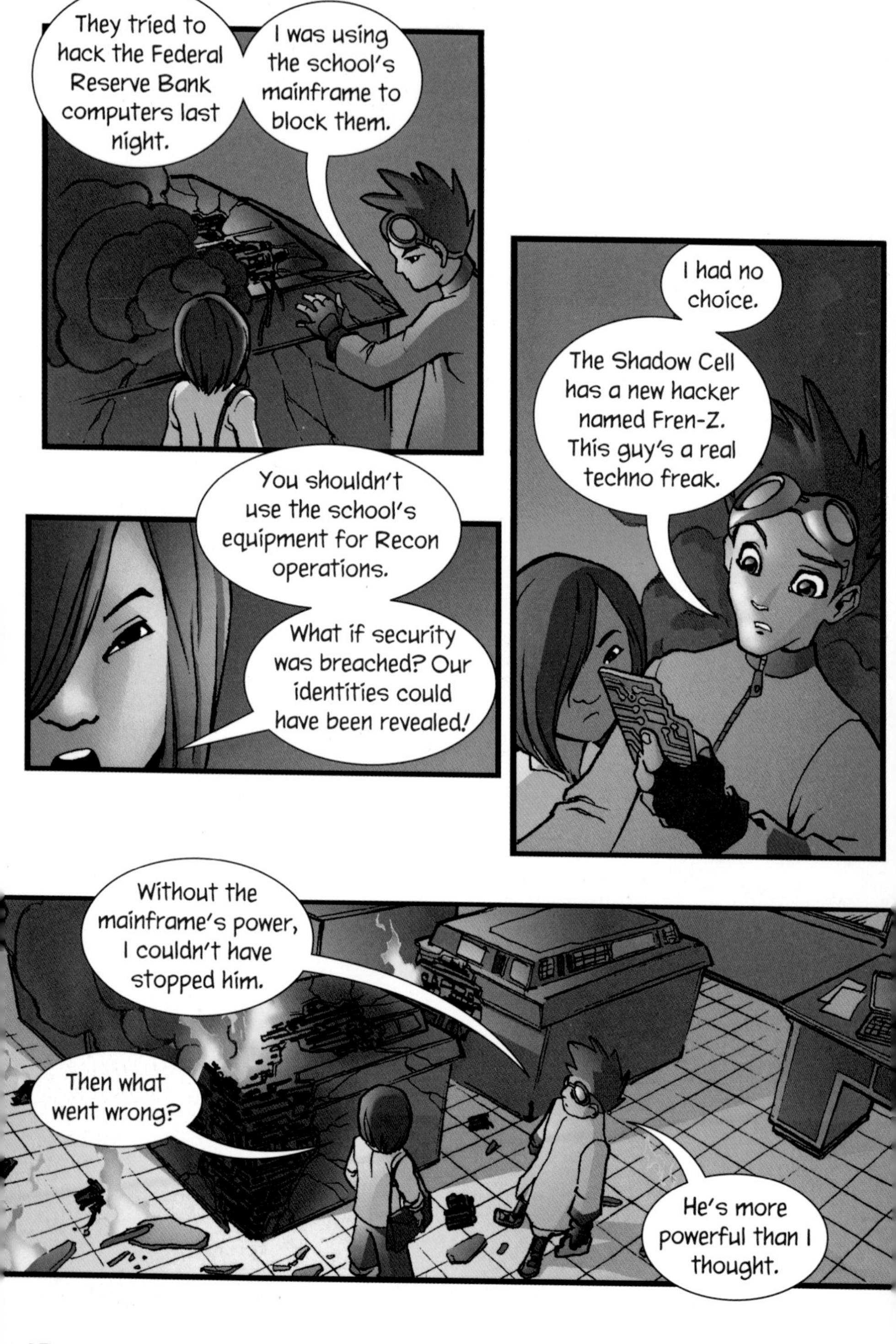

They tried to hack the Federal Reserve Bank computers last night.
I was using the school's mainframe to block them.
I had no choice.
The Shadow Cell has a new hacker named Fren-Z. This guy's a real techno freak.
You shouldn't use the school's equipment for Recon operations.
What if security was breached? Our identities could have been revealed!
Without the mainframe's power, I couldn't have stopped him.
Then what went wrong?
He's more powerful than I thought.

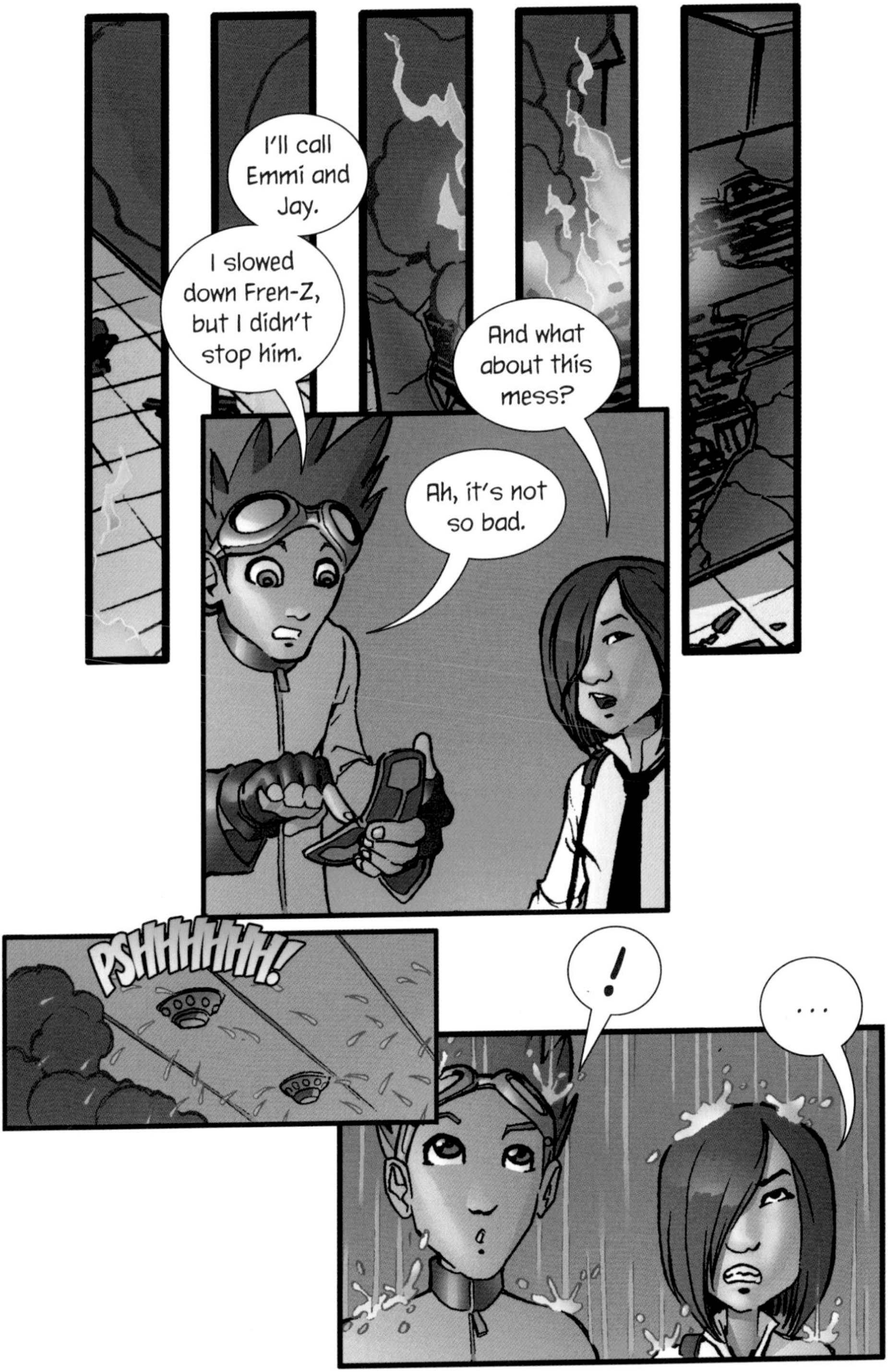
I'll call Emmi and Jay.
I slowed down Fren-Z, but I didn't stop him.
And what about this mess?
Ah, it's not so bad.
PSHHHHHH!
!
. . .

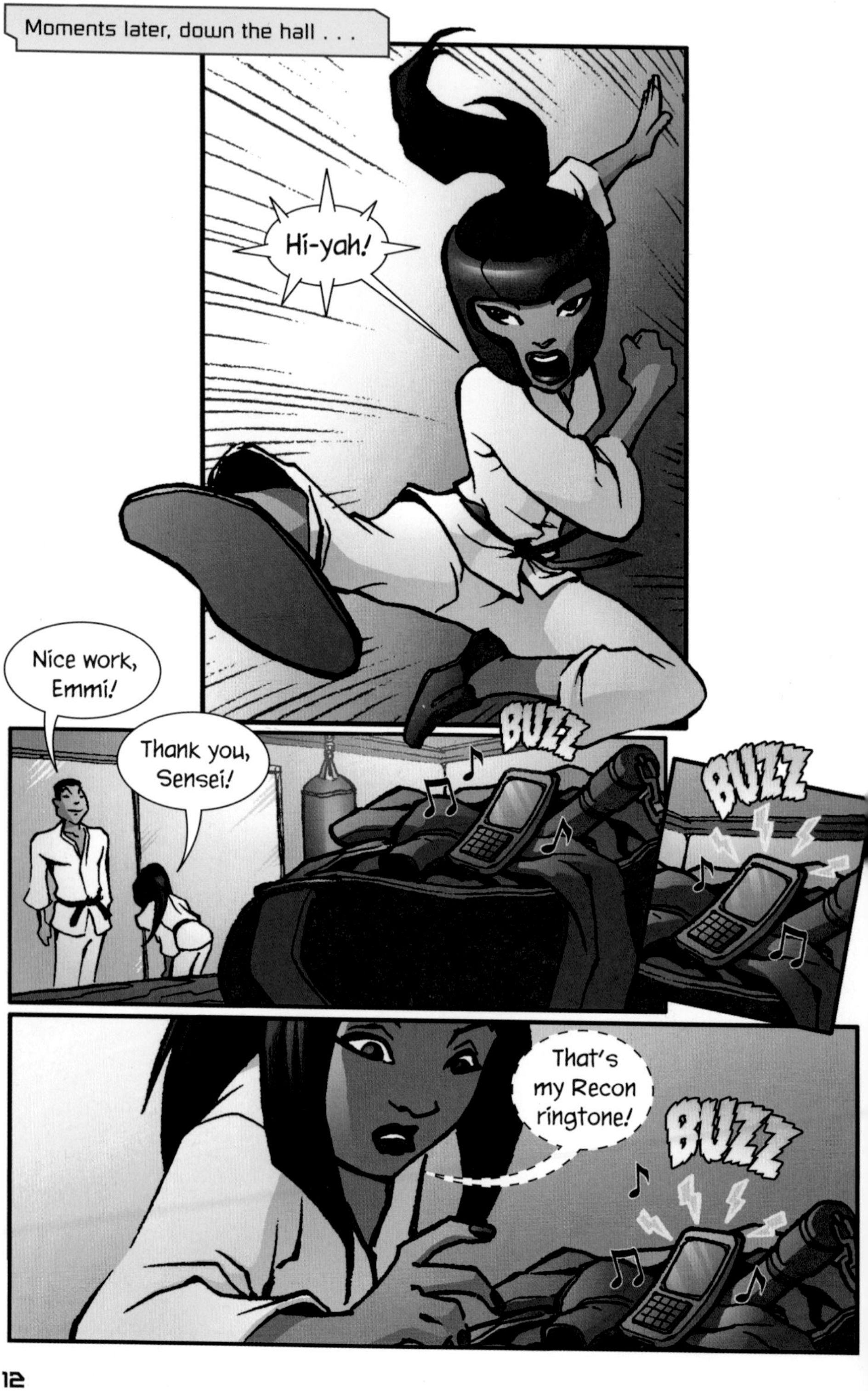
Moments later, down the hall . . .
Hi-yah!
Nice work, Emmi!
Thank you, Sensei!
BUZZ
BUZZ
That's my Recon ringtone!
BUZZ

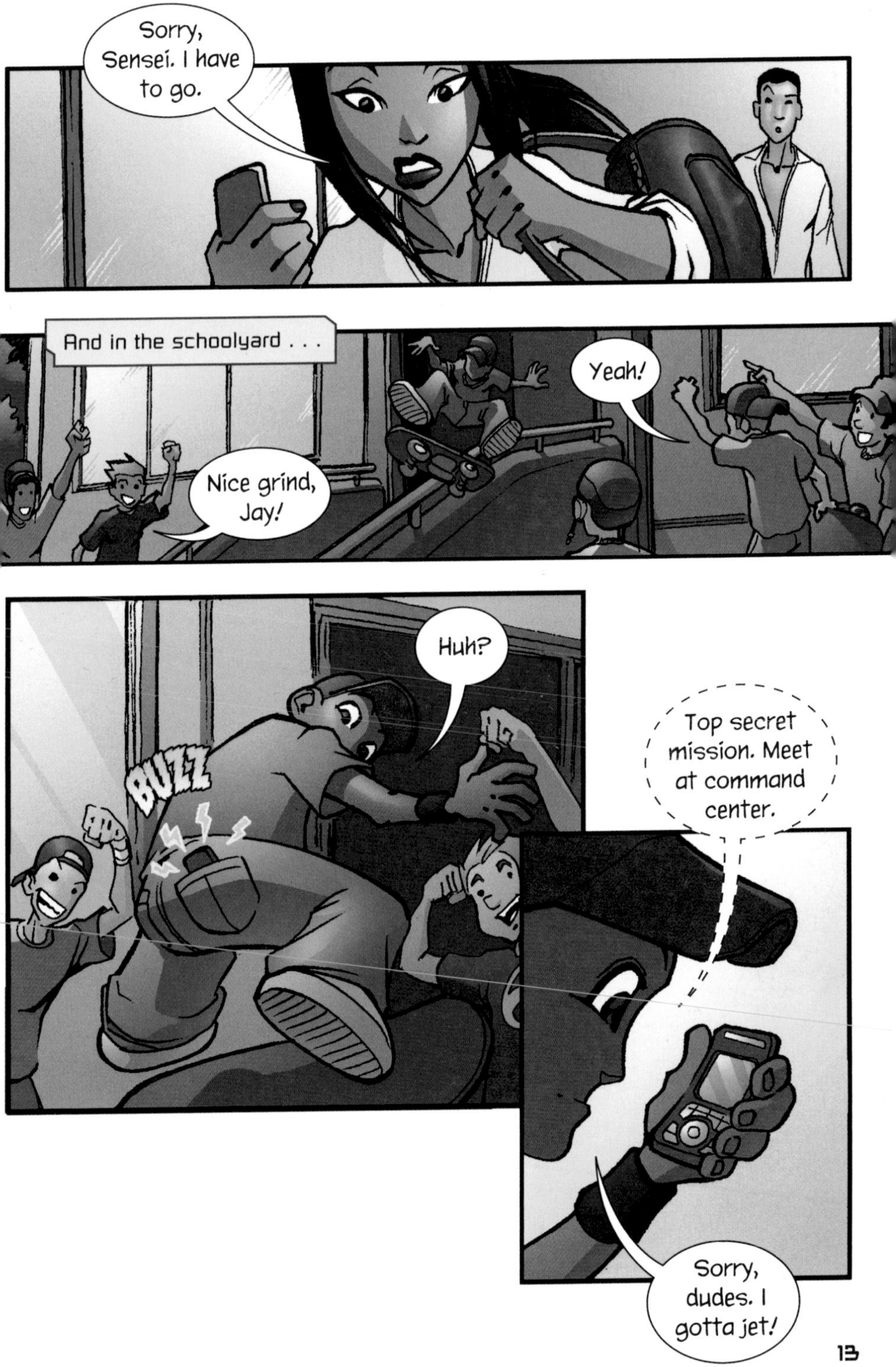
Sorry, Sensei. I have to go.
And in the schoolyard . . .
Nice grind, Jay!
Yeah!
Huh?
BUZZ
Top secret mission. Meet at command center.
Sorry, dudes. I gotta jet!

SECTION

FILE NO. 1437578

2

ACCESS GRANTED >>>>

RYKER
COMPUTERS

128718
293829
9283
98289
89
1
109201
192091
1992

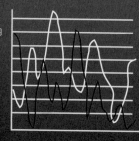

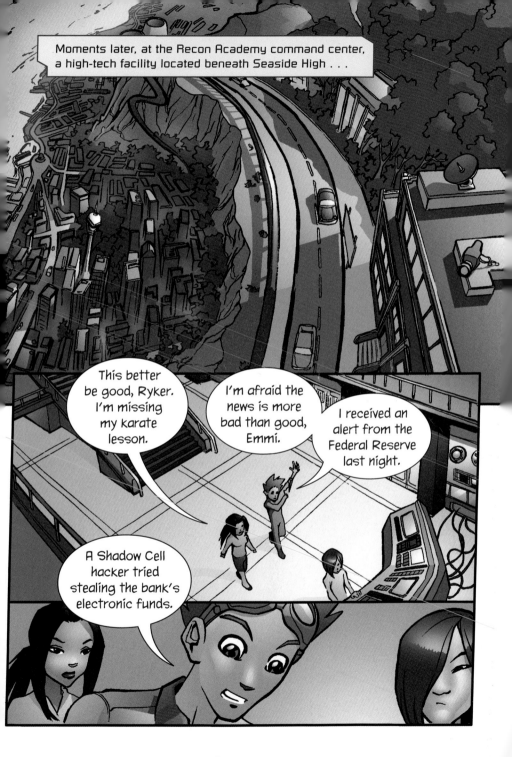

Moments later, at the Recon Academy command center, a high-tech facility located beneath Seaside High . . .

This better be good, Ryker. I'm missing my karate lesson.

I'm afraid the news is more bad than good, Emmi.

I received an alert from the Federal Reserve last night.

A Shadow Cell hacker tried stealing the bank's electronic funds.

15

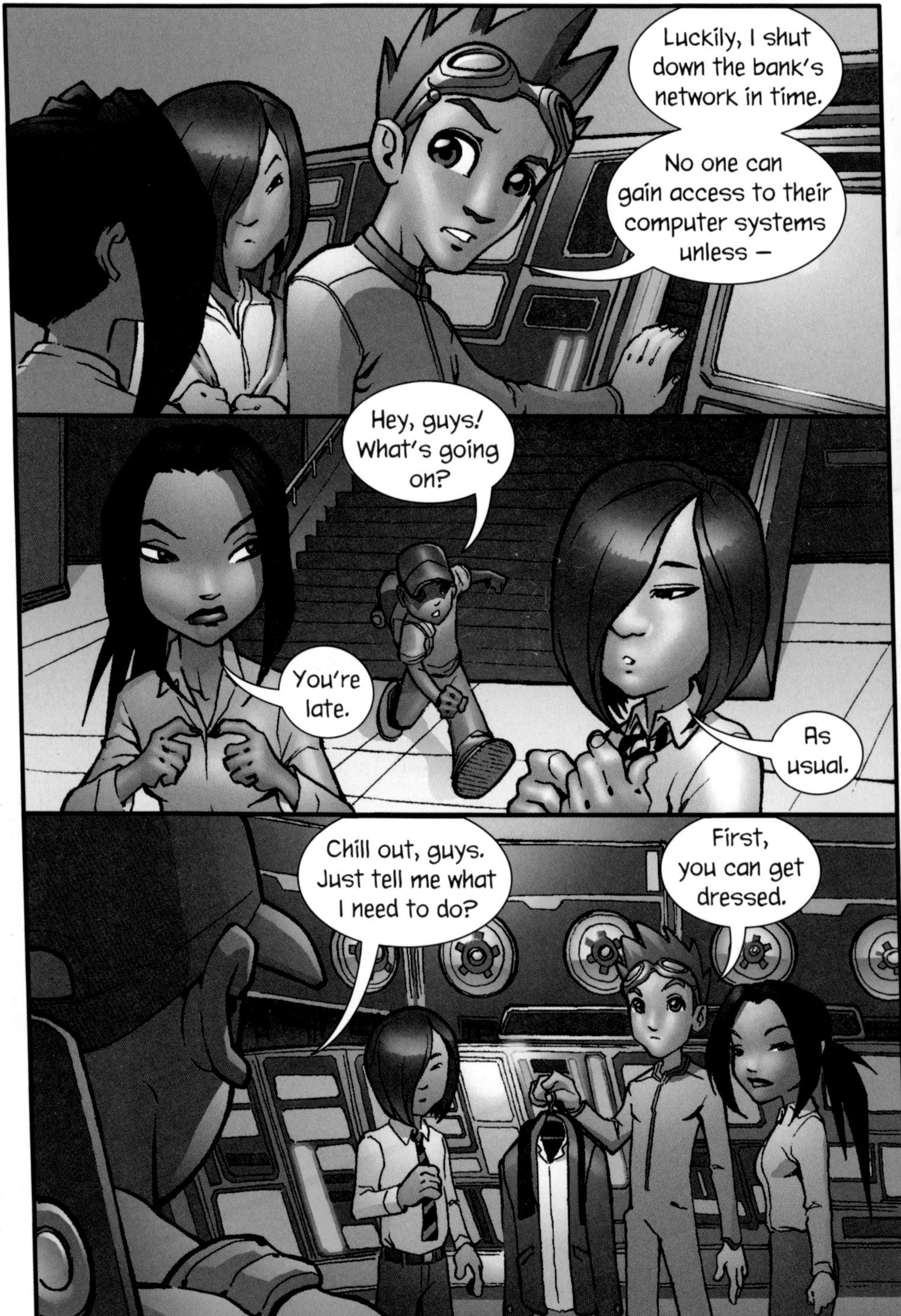
Luckily, I shut down the bank's network in time.
No one can gain access to their computer systems unless –
Hey, guys! What's going on?
You're late.
As usual.
Chill out, guys. Just tell me what I need to do?
First, you can get dressed.

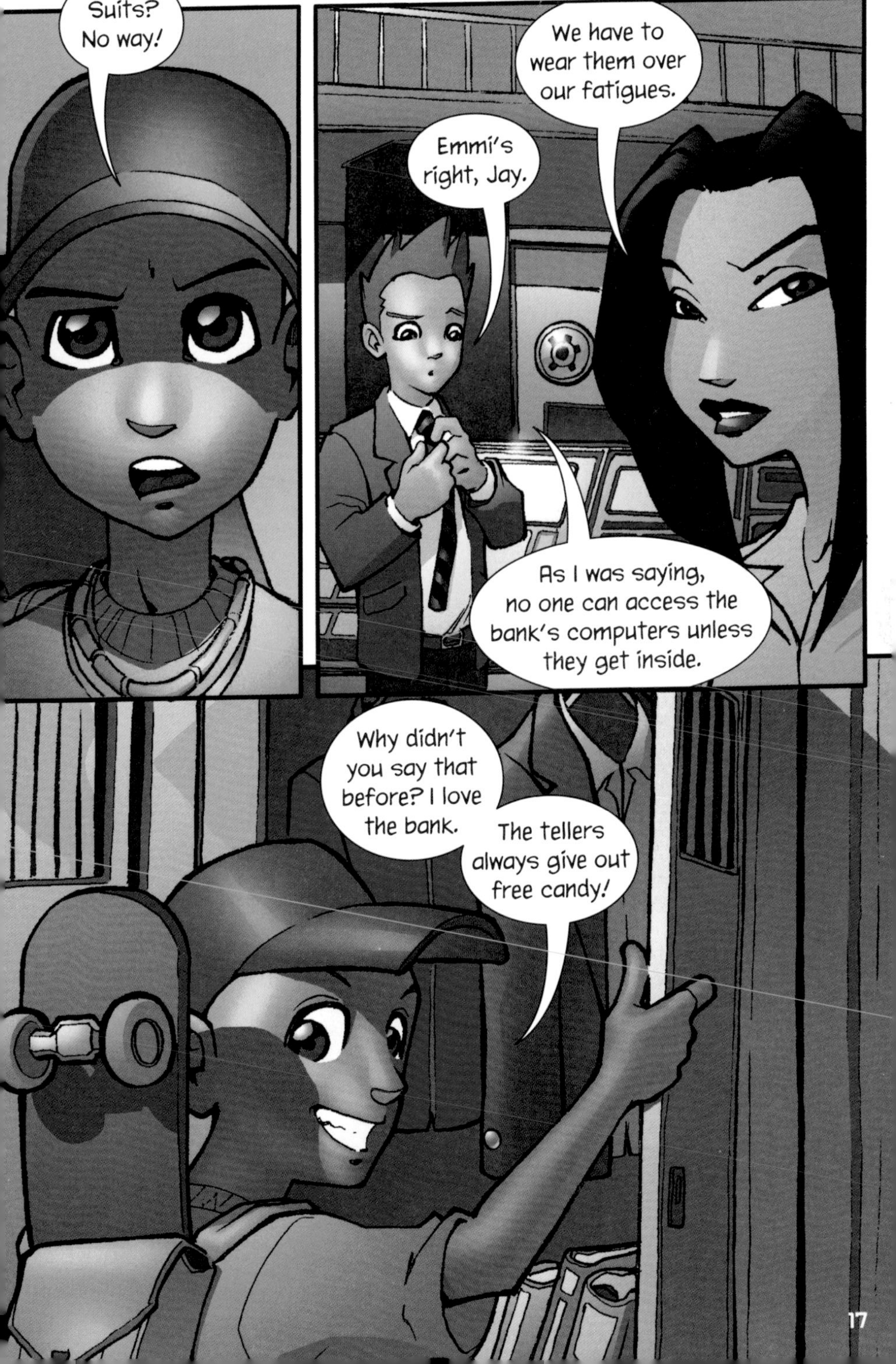

Suits? No way!
We have to wear them over our fatigues.
Emmi's right, Jay.
As I was saying, no one can access the bank's computers unless they get inside.
Why didn't you say that before? I love the bank.
The tellers always give out free candy!

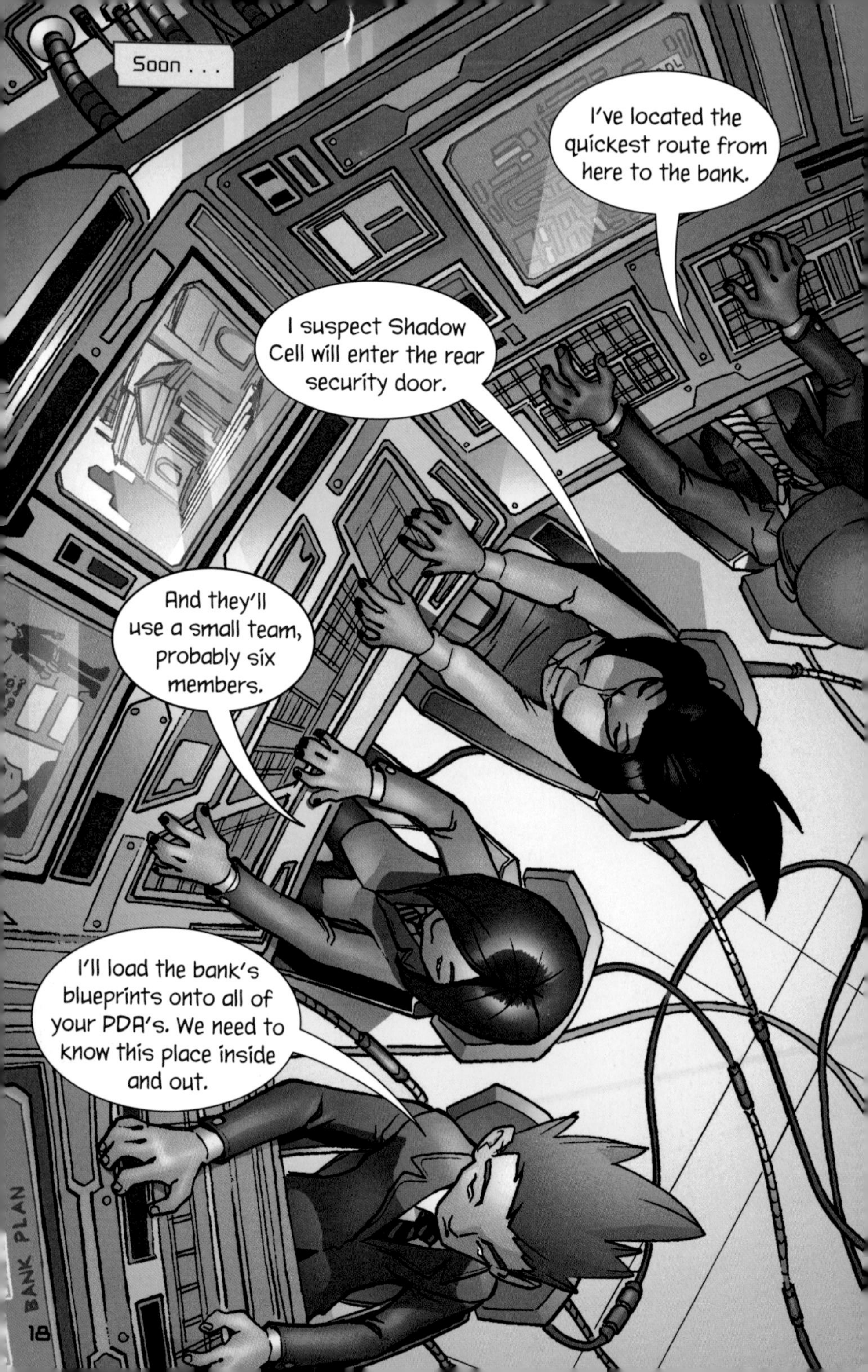
Soon . . .
I've located the quickest route from here to the bank.
I suspect Shadow Cell will enter the rear security door.
And they'll use a small team, probably six members.
I'll load the bank's blueprints onto all of your PDA's. We need to know this place inside and out.

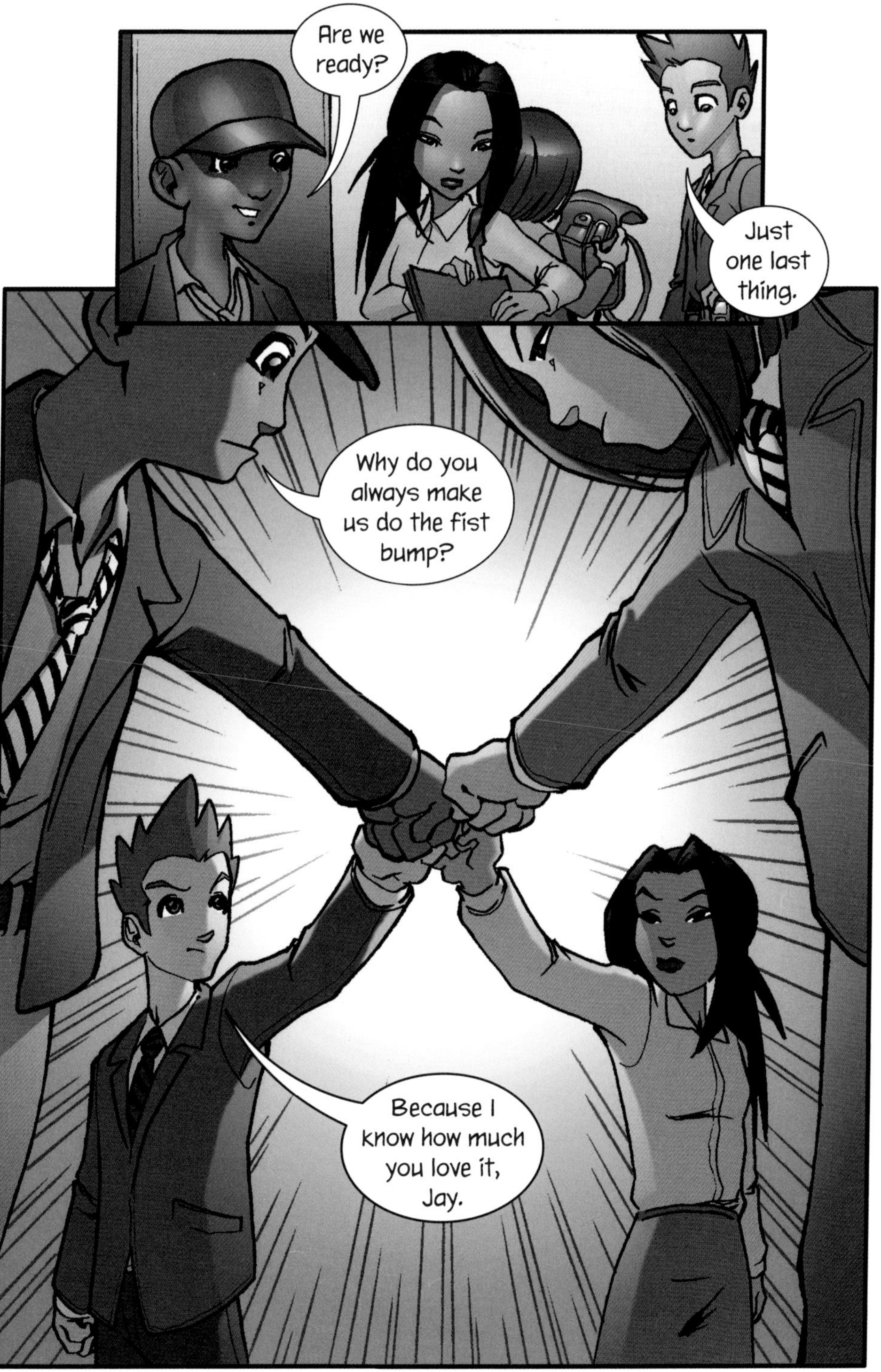
Are we ready?
Just one last thing.
Why do you always make us do the fist bump?
Because I know how much you love it, Jay.

FILE NO.
1437578

SECTION 3

ACCESS GRANTED

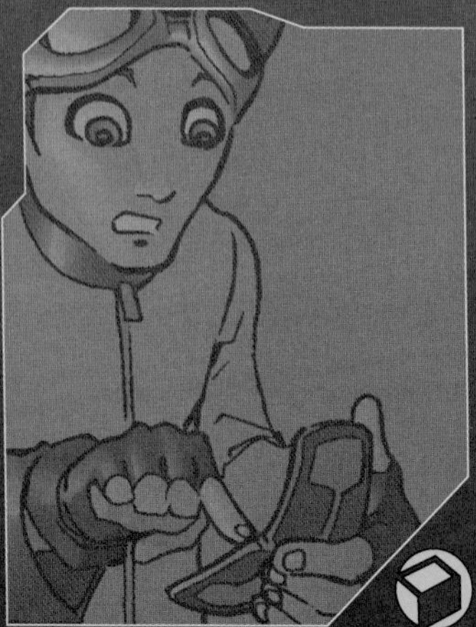

RYKER
COMPUTERS

128718
293829
9283
98289
89
1
109201
192091
1992

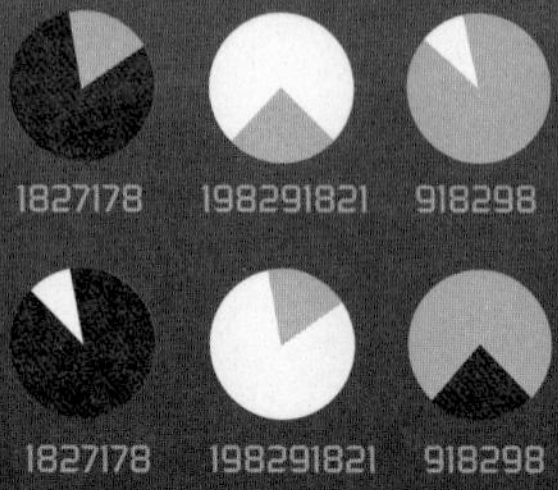

1827178
198291821
918298
1827178
198291821
918298

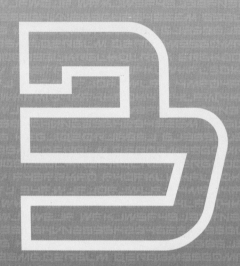

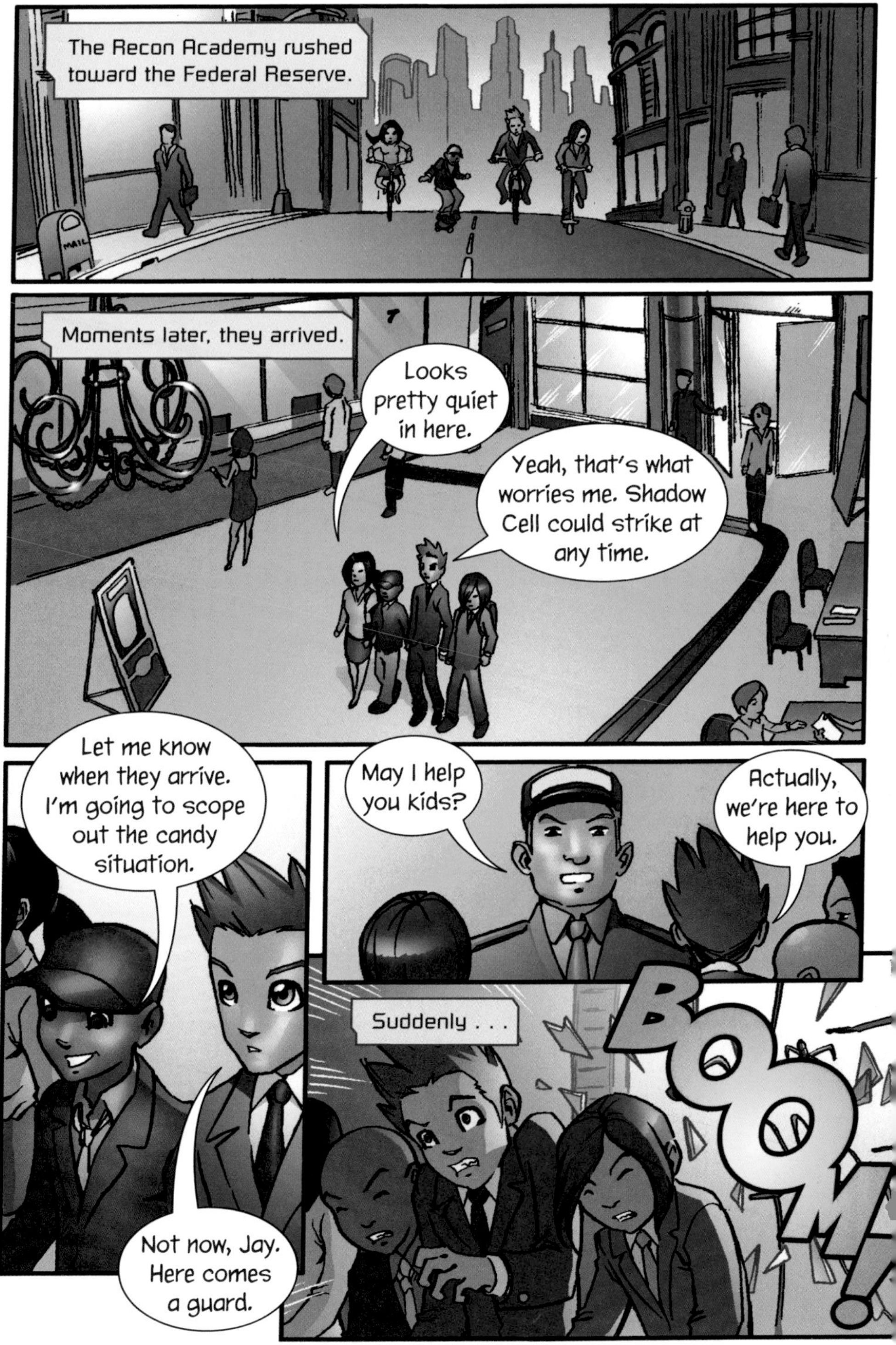
The Recon Academy rushed toward the Federal Reserve.
MAIL
Moments later, they arrived.
Looks pretty quiet in here.
Yeah, that's what worries me. Shadow Cell could strike at any time.
Let me know when they arrive. I'm going to scope out the candy situation.
Not now, Jay. Here comes a guard.
May I help you kids?
Actually, we're here to help you.
Suddenly . . .
BOOM!

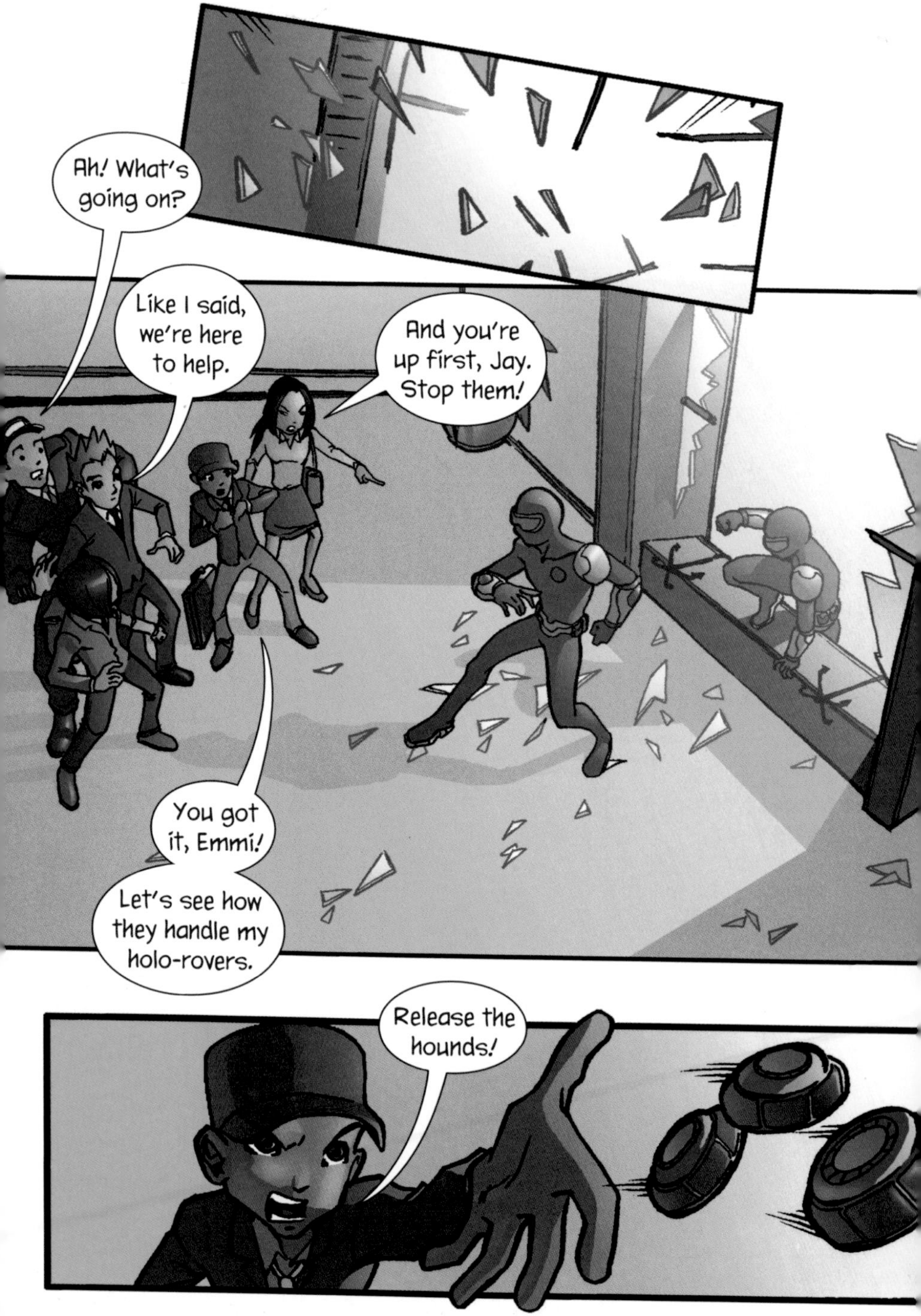

Ah! What's going on?
Like I said, we're here to help.
And you're up first, Jay. Stop them!
You got it, Emmi!
Let's see how they handle my holo-rovers.
Release the hounds!

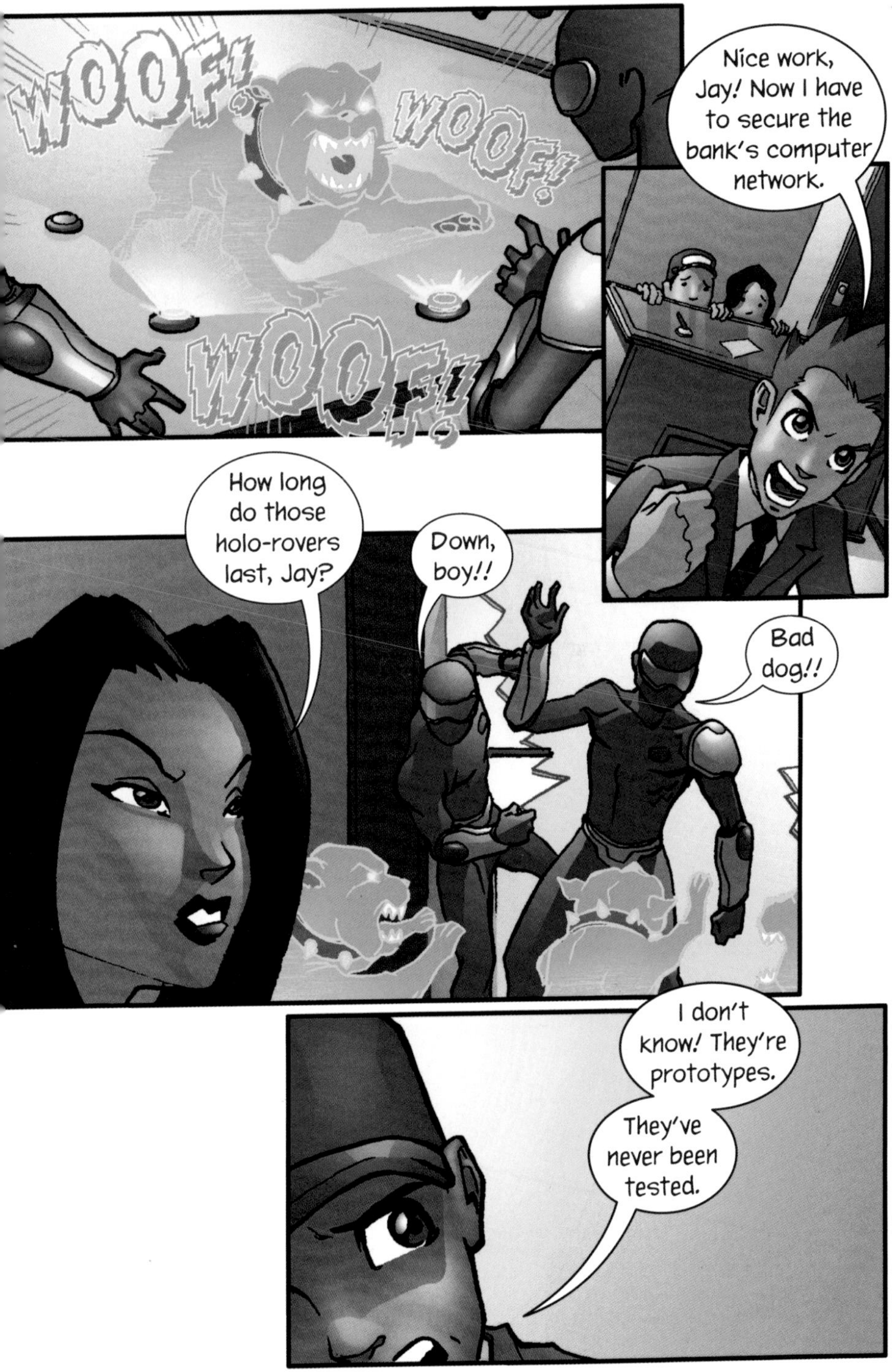
WOOF!
WOOF!
WOOF!
Nice work, Jay! Now I have to secure the bank's computer network.
How long do those holo-rovers last, Jay?
Down, boy!!
Bad dog!!
I don't know! They're prototypes.
They've never been tested.

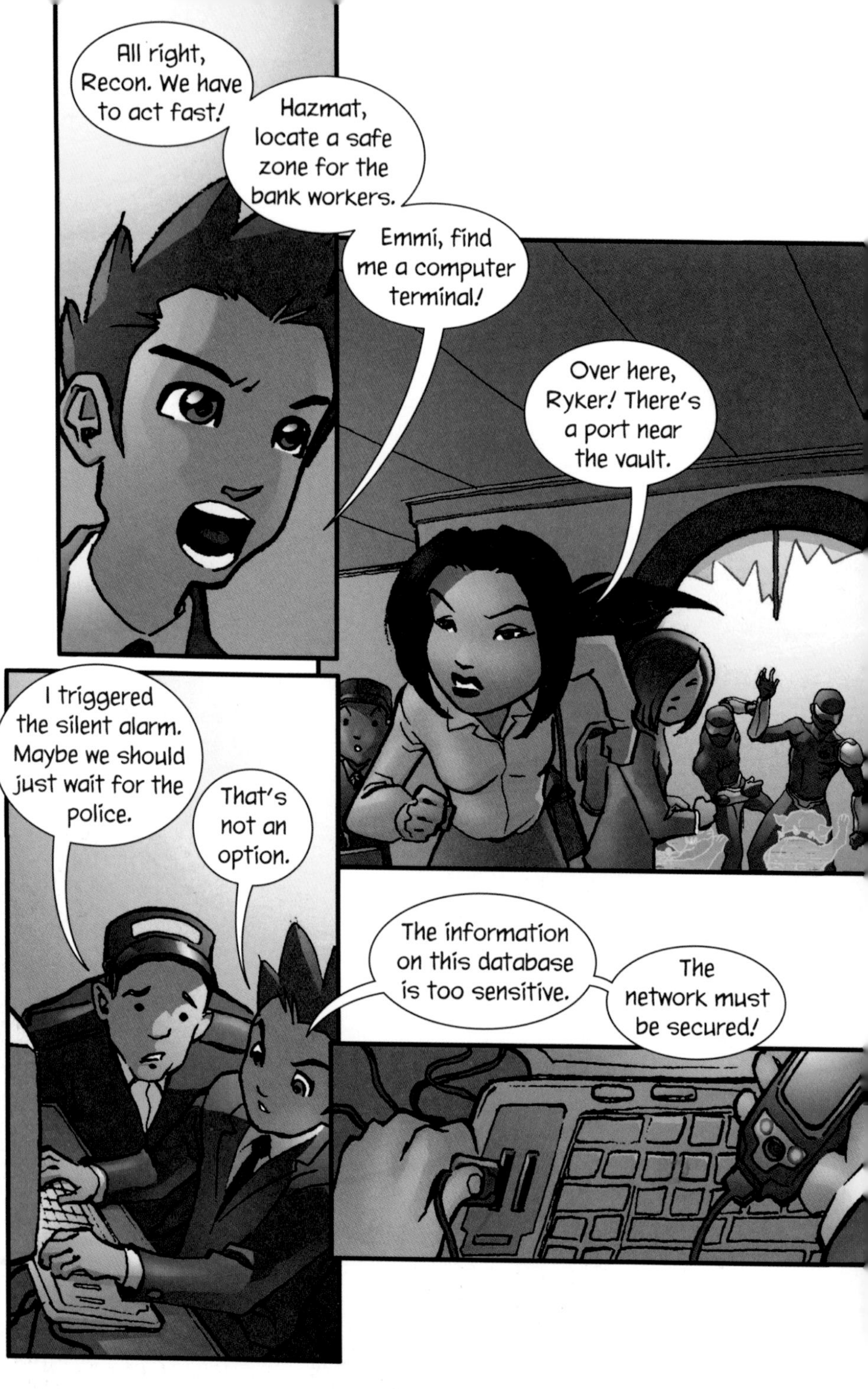
All right, Recon. We have to act fast!
Hazmat, locate a safe zone for the bank workers.
Emmi, find me a computer terminal!
Over here, Ryker! There's a port near the vault.
I triggered the silent alarm. Maybe we should just wait for the police.
That's not an option.
The information on this database is too sensitive.
The network must be secured!

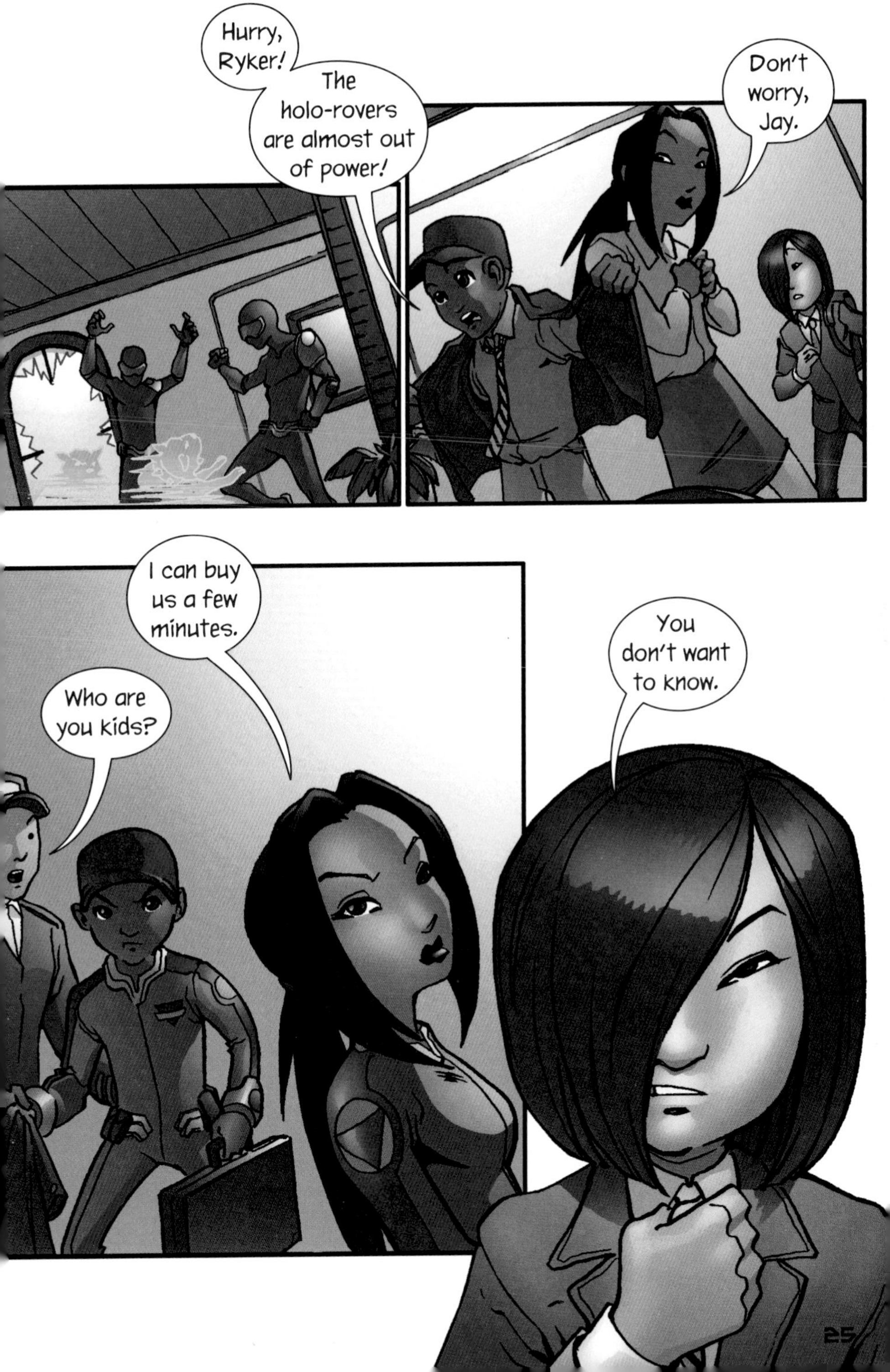

Hurry, Ryker!
The holo-rovers are almost out of power!
Don't worry, Jay.
I can buy us a few minutes.
Who are you kids?
You don't want to know.

SECTION

FILE NO. 1437578

4

ACCESS GRANTED >>>>

RYKER
COMPUTERS

8579
1564574
109201
192091
1992
745979

128718
293829
9283
68286
98
1
109201
192091
1992

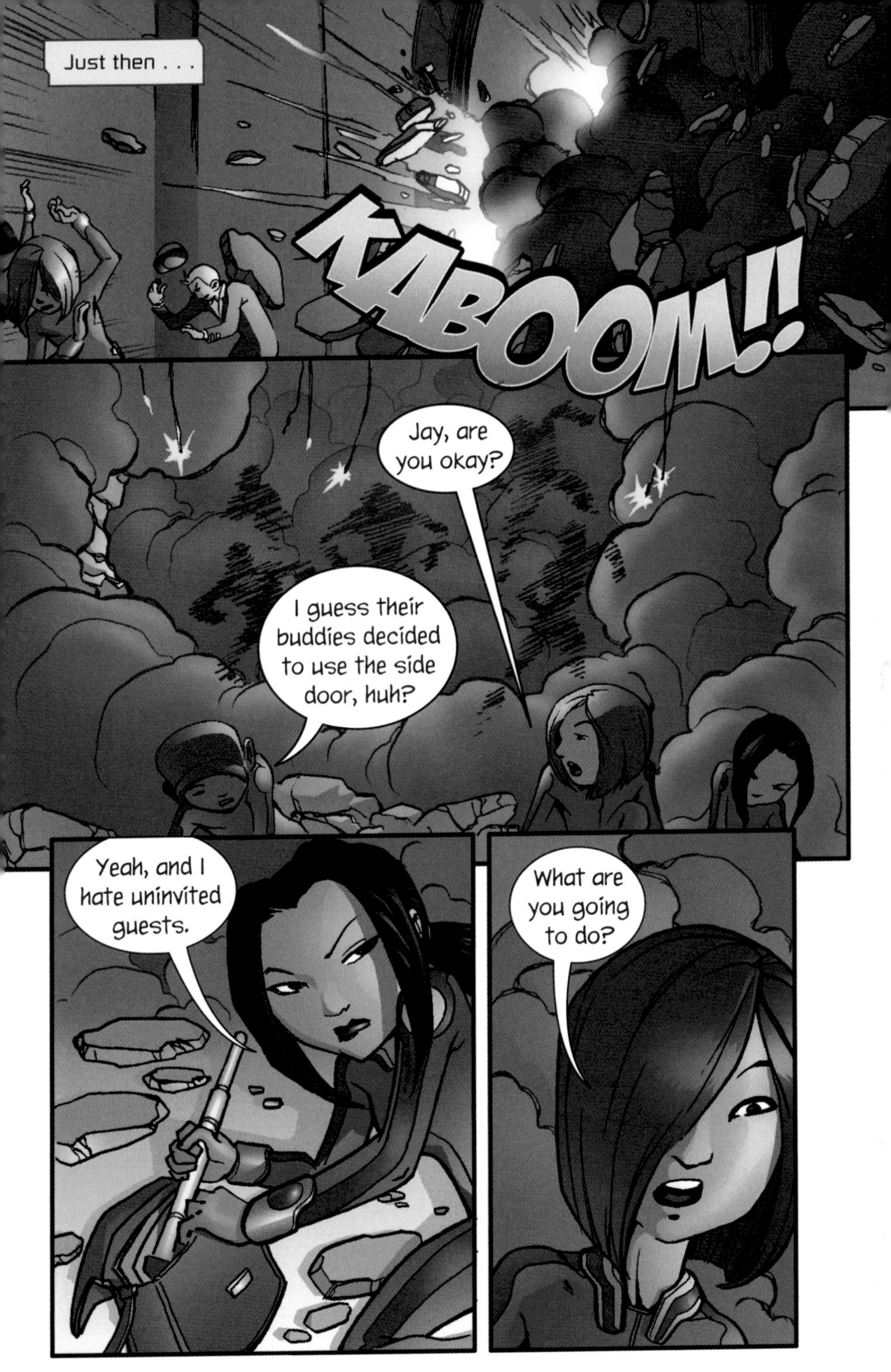
Just then . . .
KABOOM!!
Jay, are you okay?
I guess their buddies decided to use the side door, huh?
Yeah, and I hate uninvited guests.
What are you going to do?

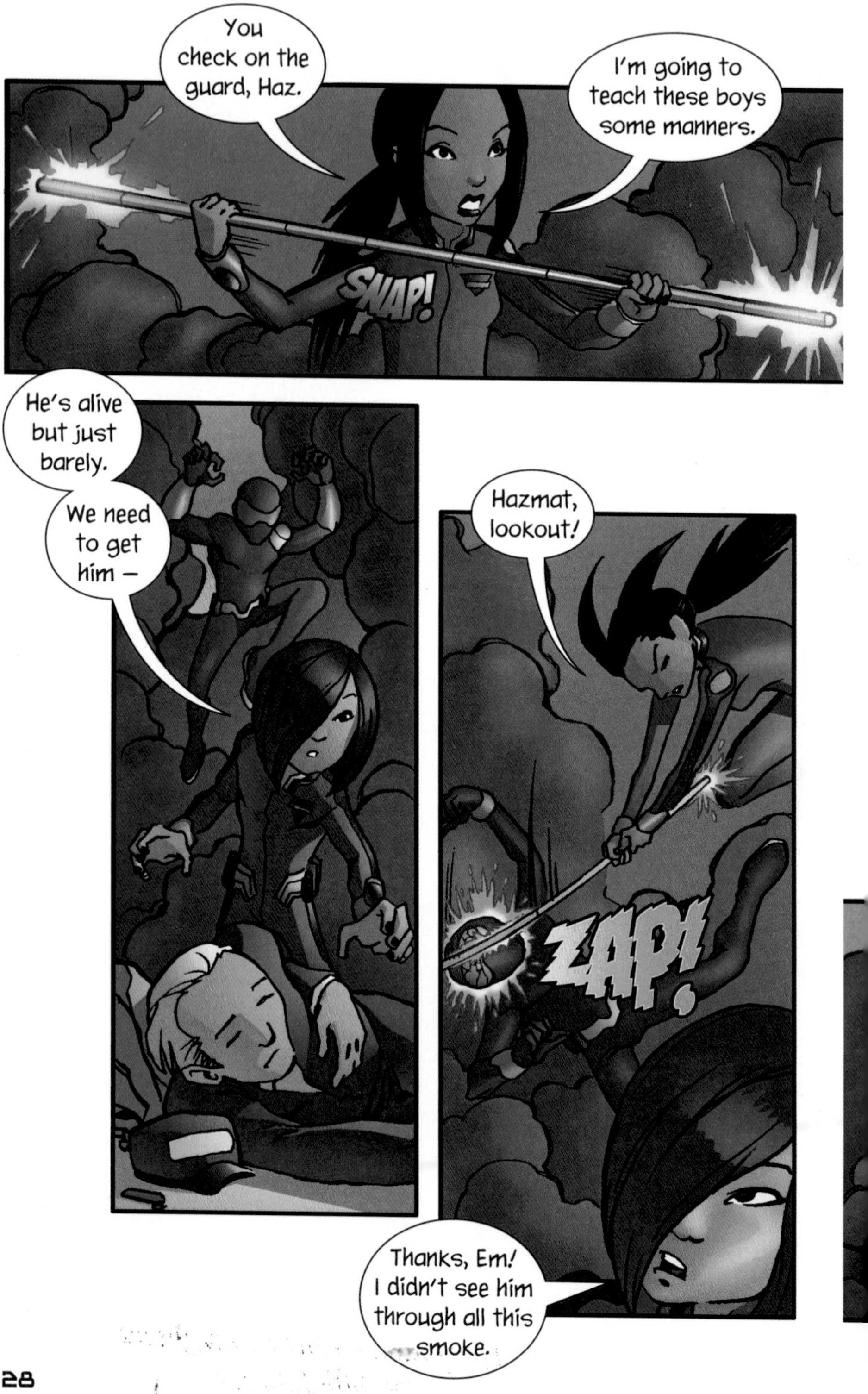
You check on the guard, Haz.
I'm going to teach these boys some manners.
SNAP!
He's alive but just barely.
We need to get him –
Hazmat, lookout!
ZAP!
Thanks, Em! I didn't see him through all this smoke.

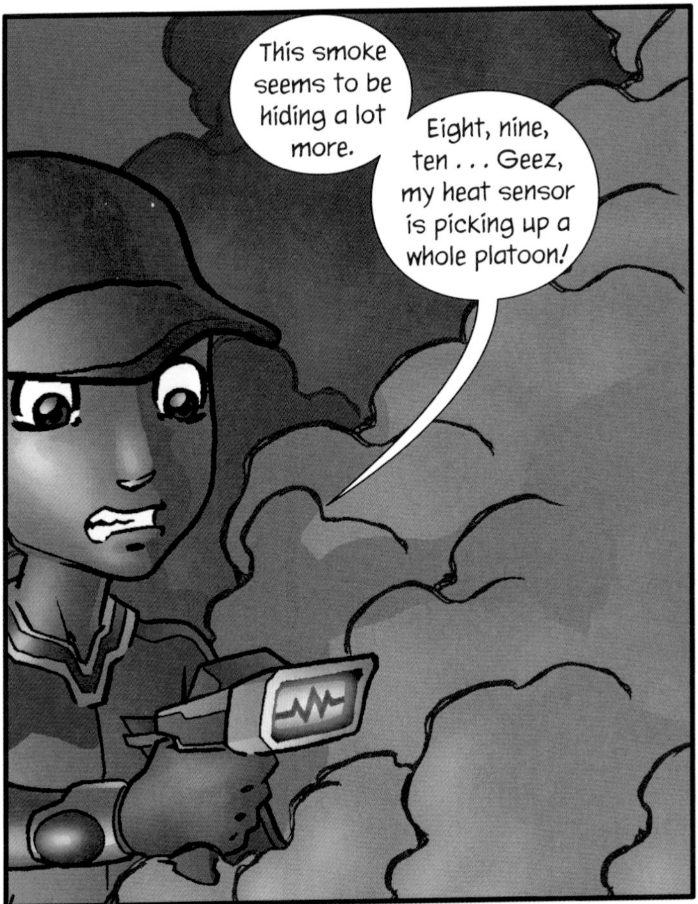
This smoke seems to be hiding a lot more.
Eight, nine, ten . . . Geez, my heat sensor is picking up a whole platoon!

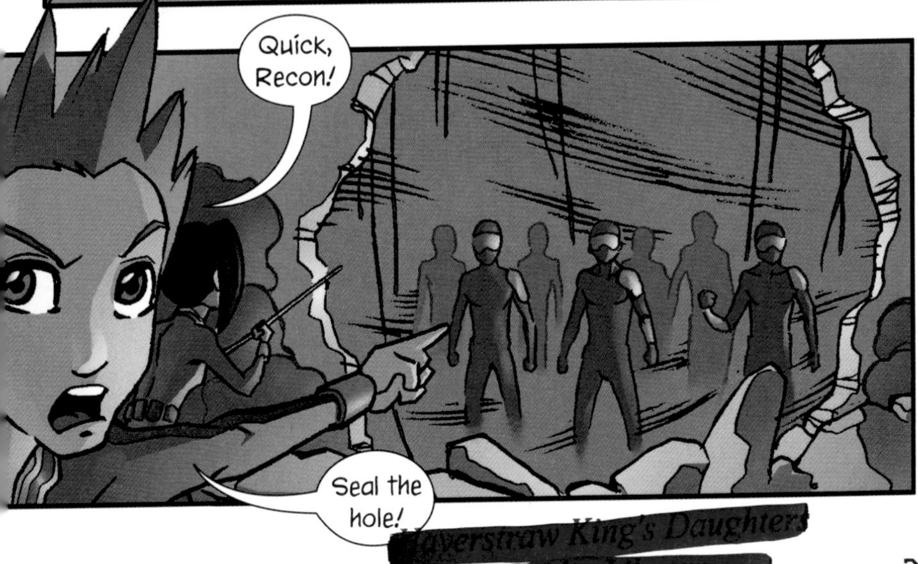
Quick, Recon!
Seal the hole!

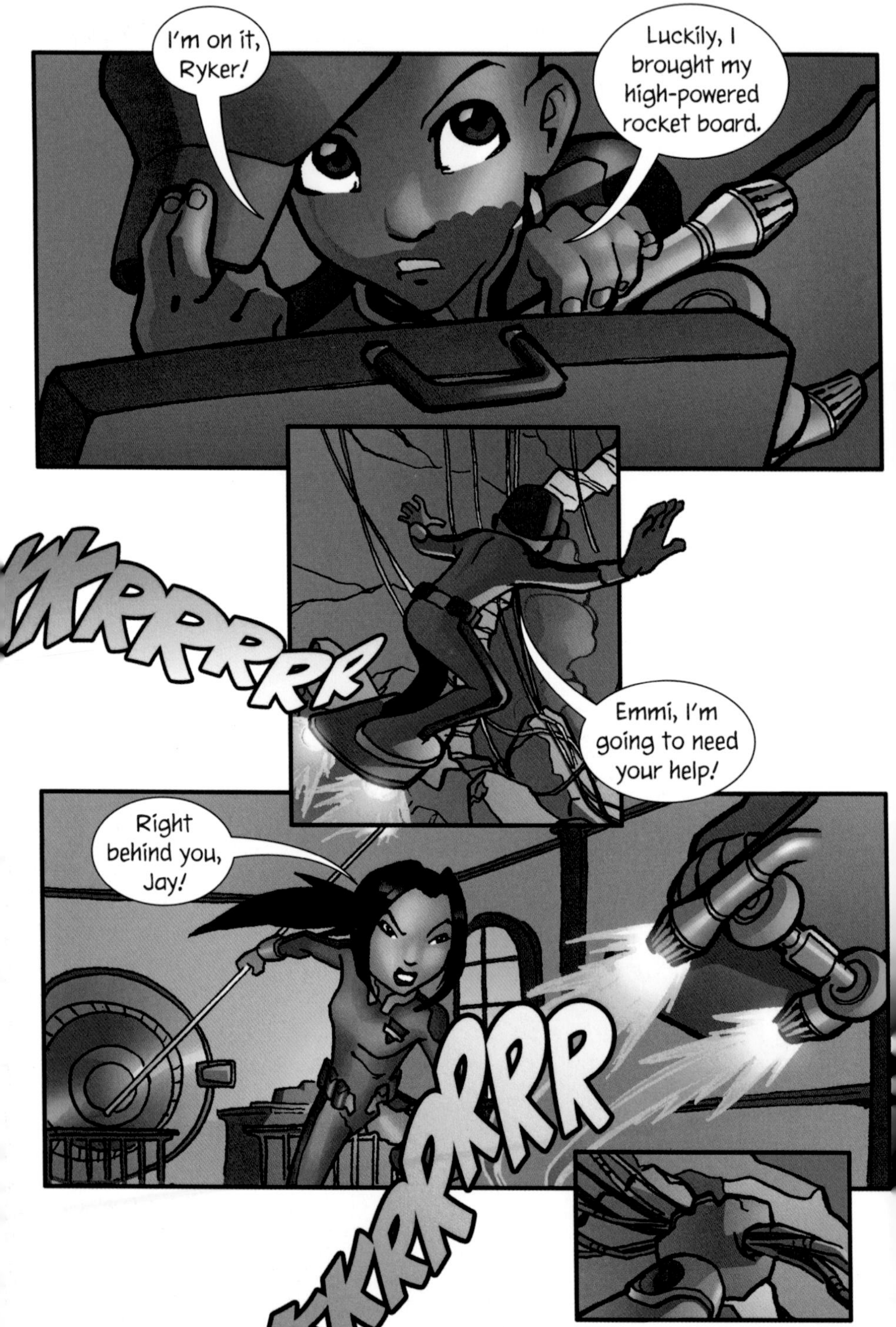
I'm on it, Ryker!
Luckily, I brought my high-powered rocket board.
Emmi, I'm going to need your help!
Right behind you, Jay!

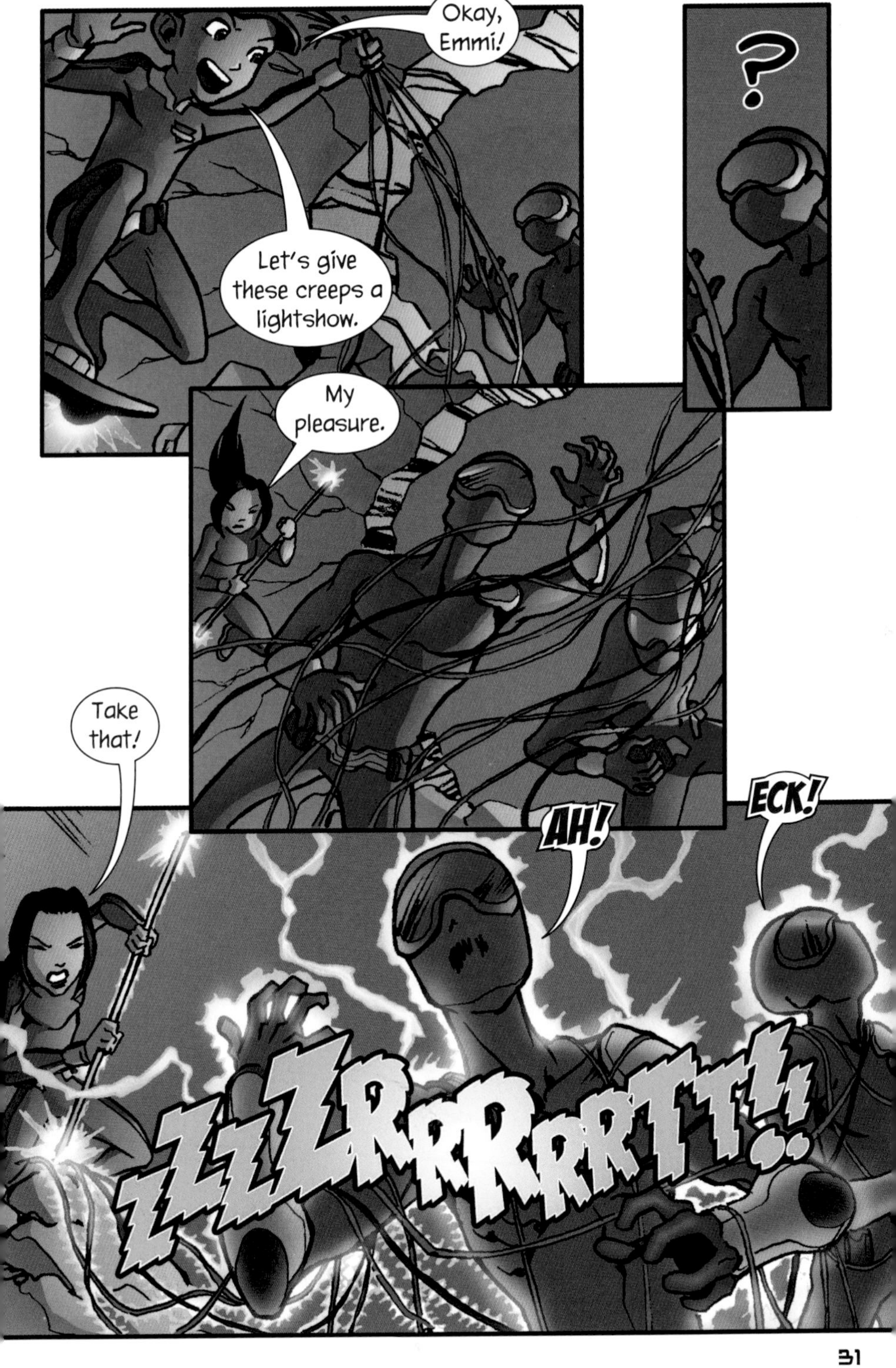
Okay, Emmi!
Let's give these creeps a lightshow.
?
My pleasure.
Take that!
AH!
ECK!
ZZZZRRRRRRTTT!!

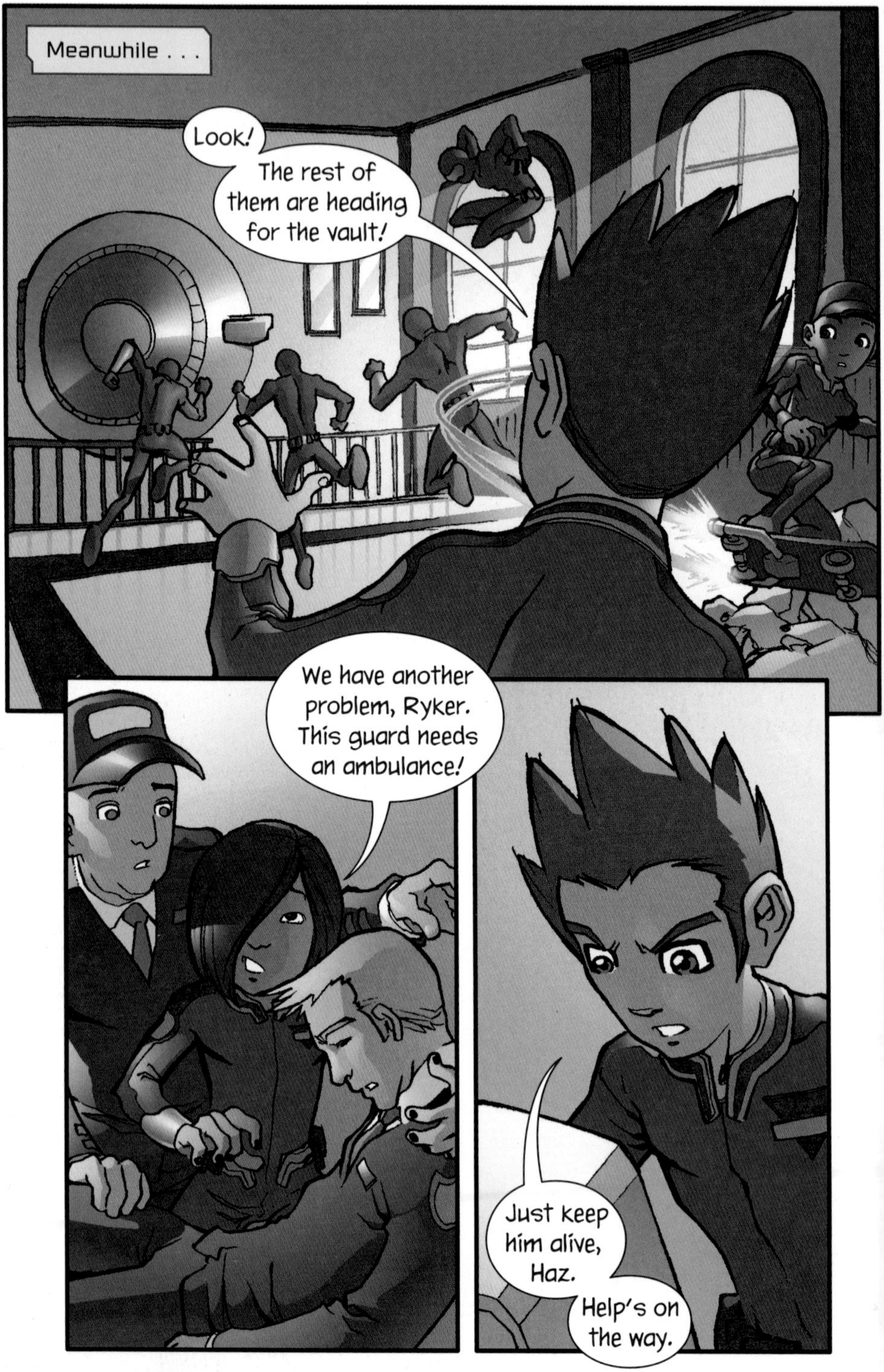
Meanwhile . . .
Look!
The rest of them are heading for the vault!
We have another problem, Ryker. This guard needs an ambulance!
Just keep him alive, Haz.
Help's on the way.

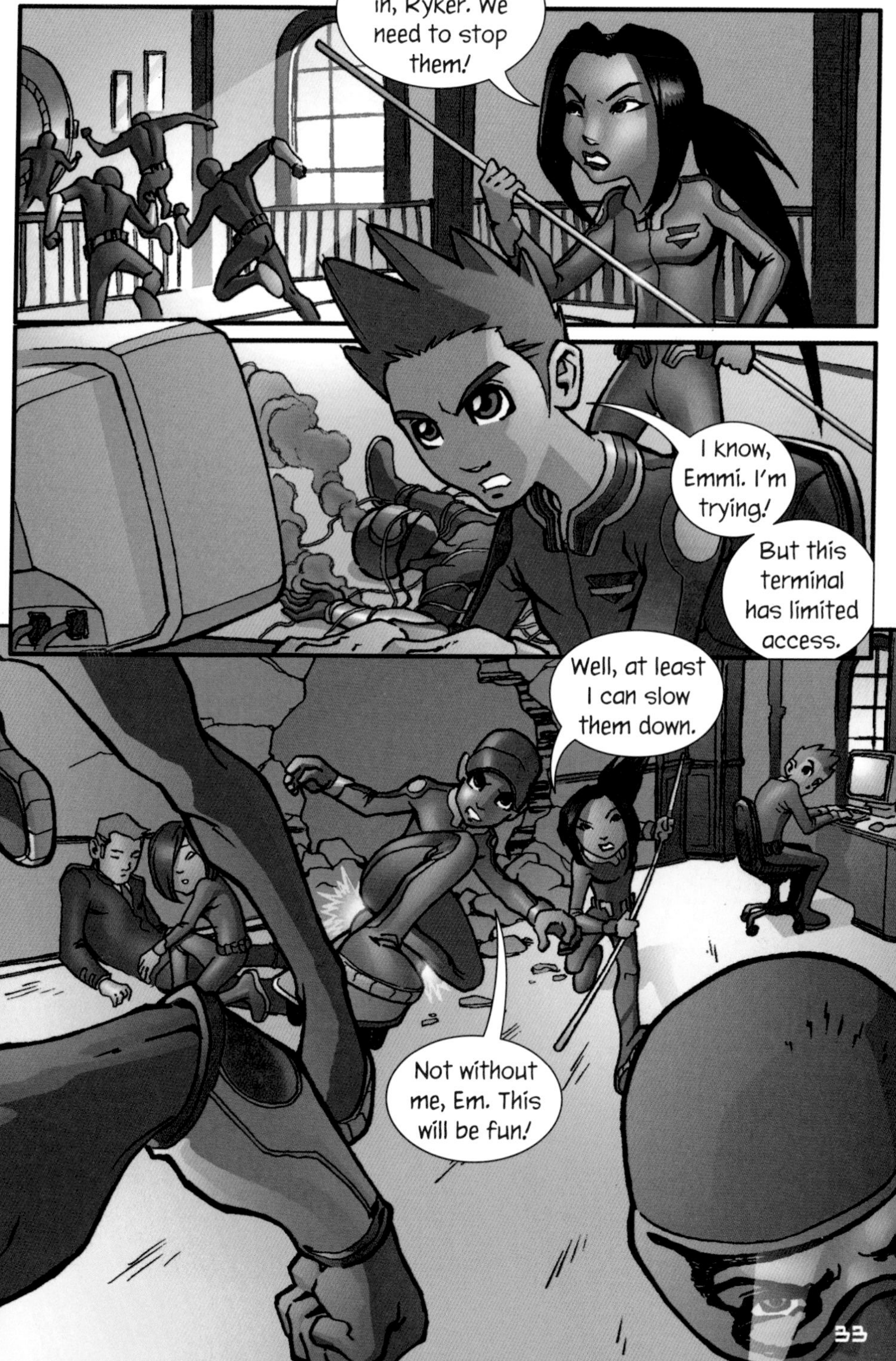
They're almost in, Ryker. We need to stop them!
I know, Emmi. I'm trying!
But this terminal has limited access.
Well, at least I can slow them down.
Not without me, Em. This will be fun!

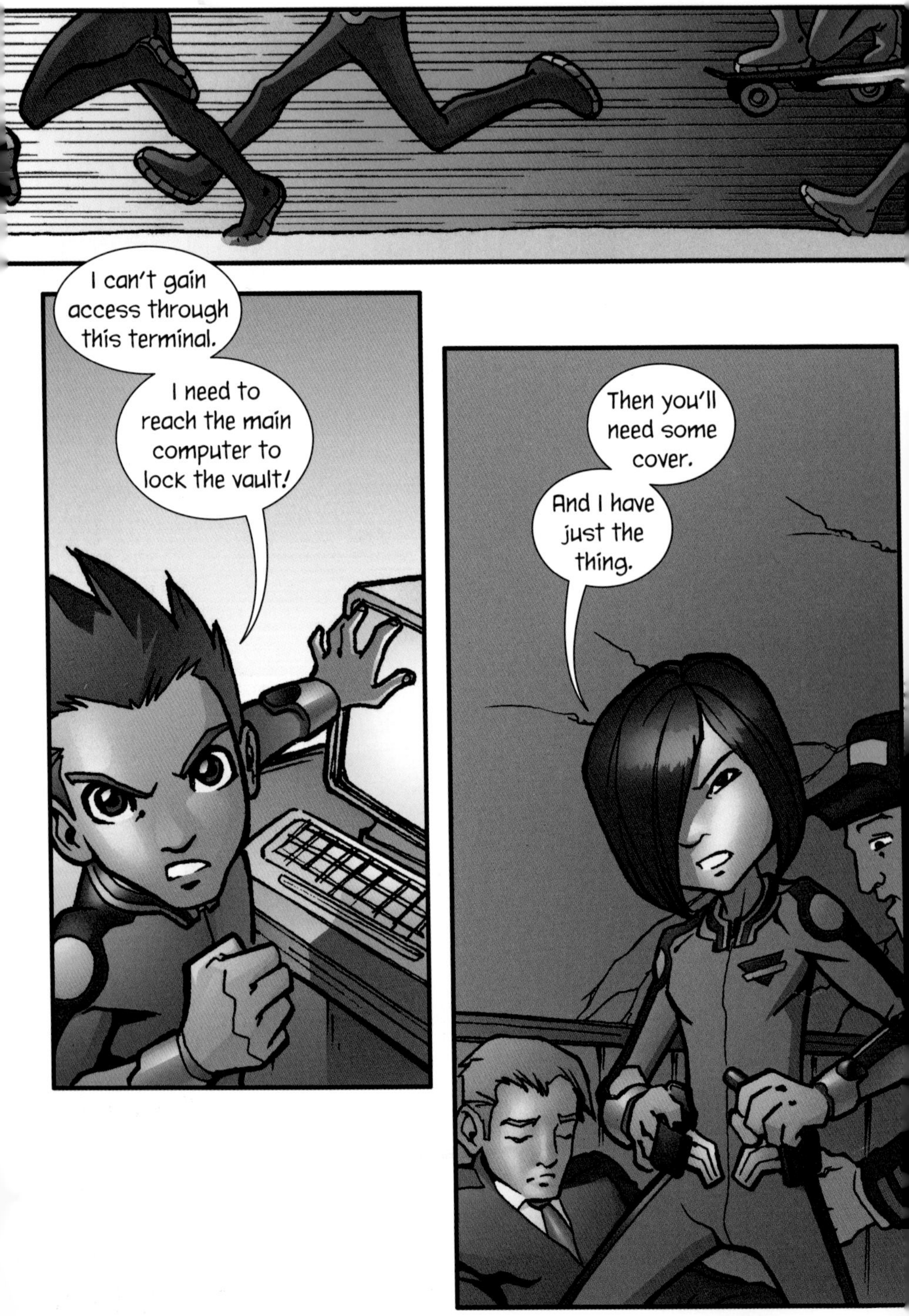
I can't gain access through this terminal.
I need to reach the main computer to lock the vault!
Then you'll need some cover.
And I have just the thing.

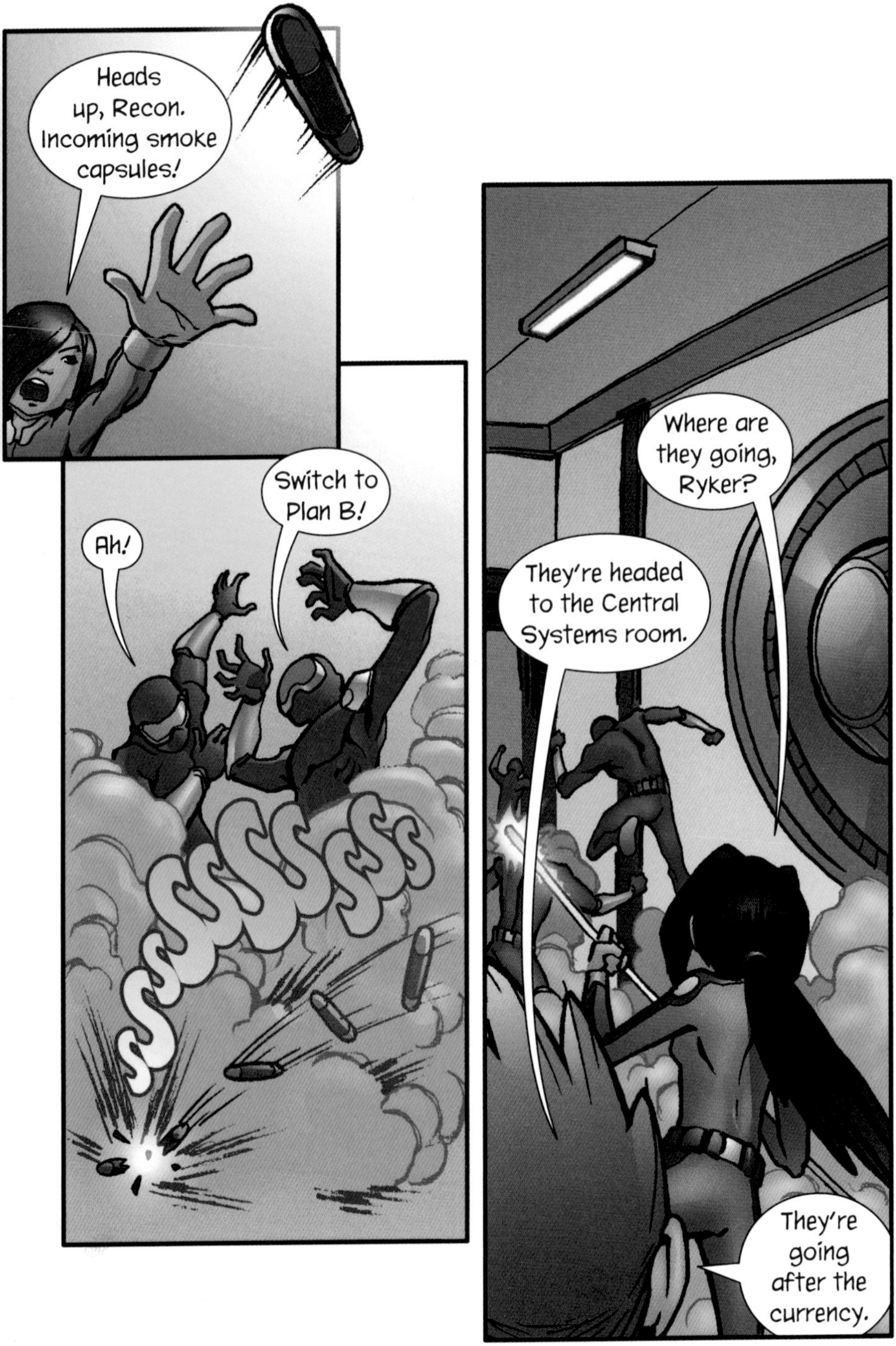
Heads up, Recon. Incoming smoke capsules!
Ah!
Switch to Plan B!
SSSSSSSSSSS
Where are they going, Ryker?
They're headed to the Central Systems room.
They're going after the currency.

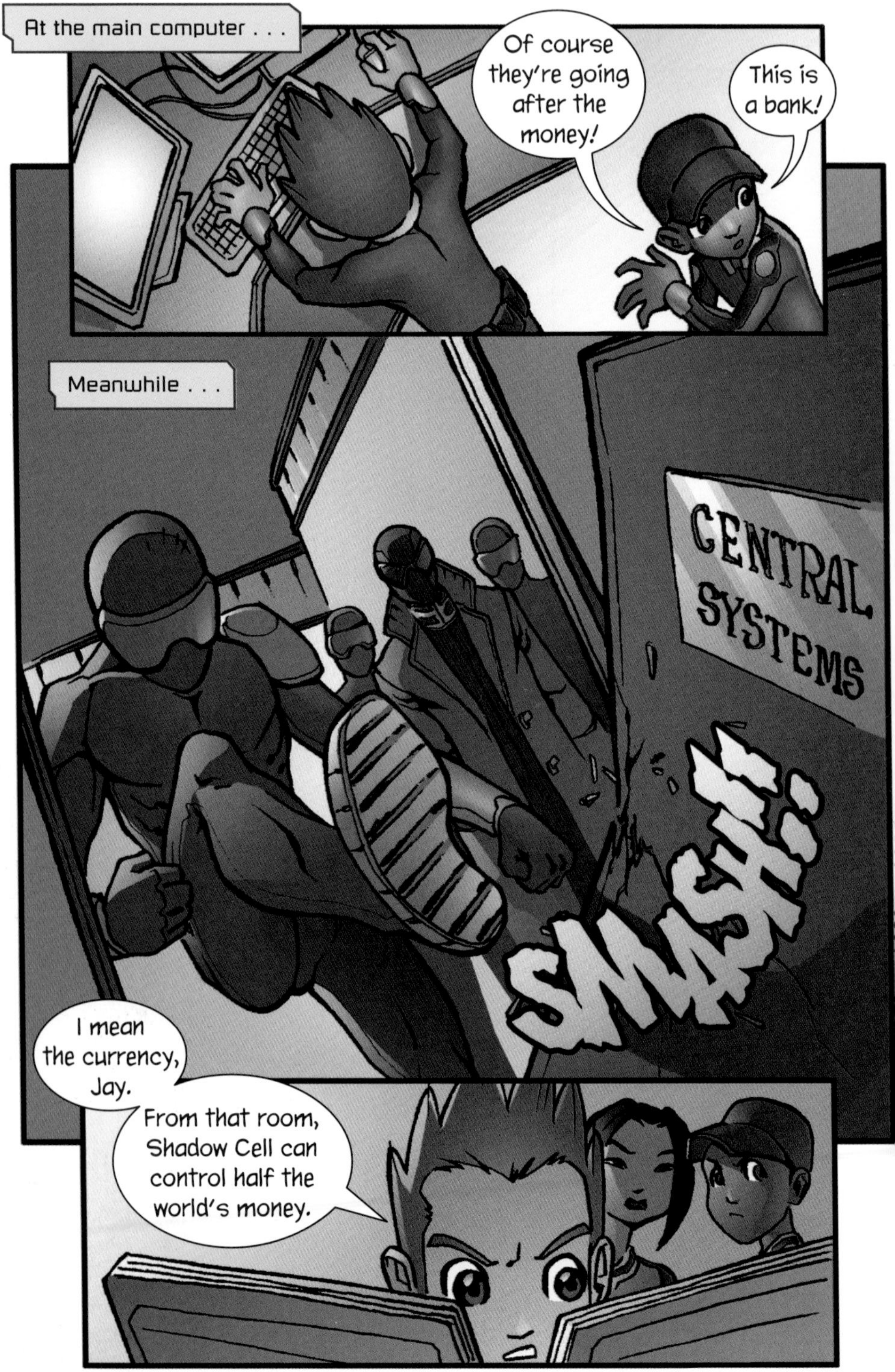
At the main computer . . .
Of course they're going after the money!
This is a bank!
Meanwhile . . .
CENTRAL SYSTEMS
SMASH!
I mean the currency, Jay.
From that room, Shadow Cell can control half the world's money.

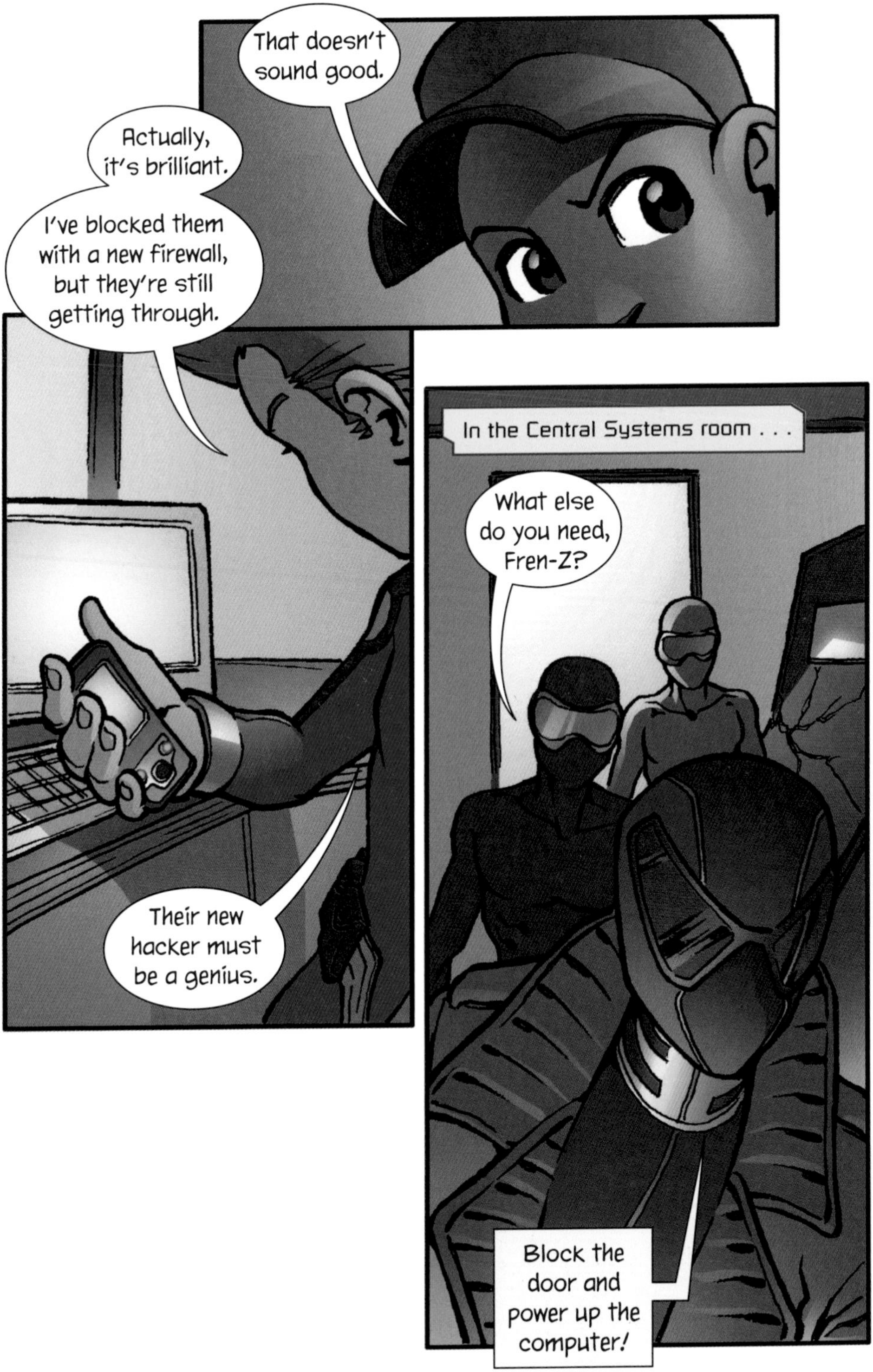
That doesn't sound good.
Actually, it's brilliant.
I've blocked them with a new firewall, but they're still getting through.
Their new hacker must be a genius.
In the Central Systems room . . .
What else do you need, Fren-Z?
Block the door and power up the computer!

SECTION

5

ACCESS GRANTED >>>>

FILE NO. 1437578

RYKER
COMPUTERS

128718
293829
9283
98289
89
1
109201
192091
1992

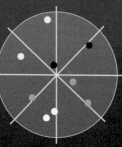

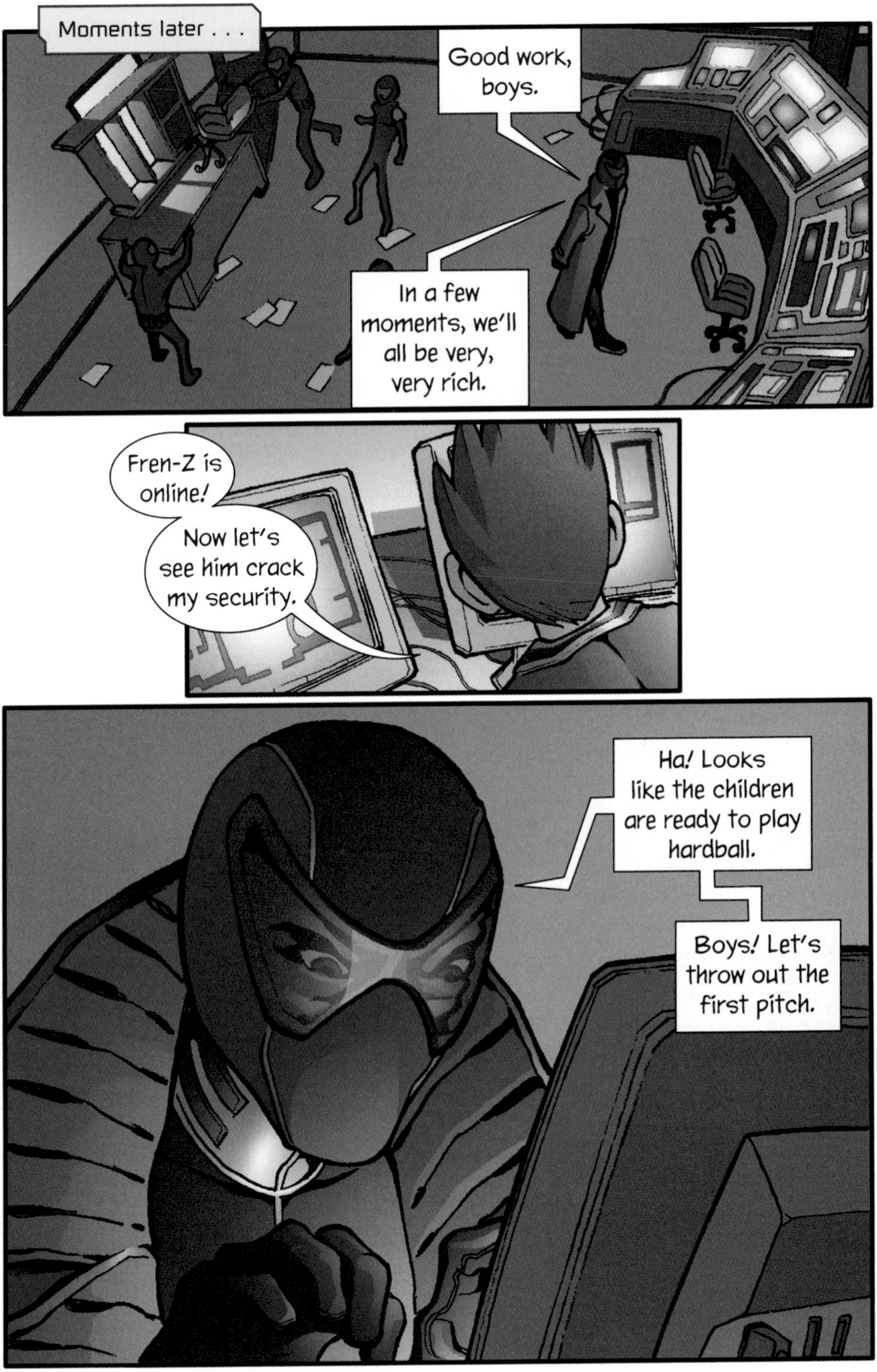
Moments later . . .
Good work, boys.
In a few moments, we'll all be very, very rich.
Fren-Z is online!
Now let's see him crack my security.
Ha! Looks like the children are ready to play hardball.
Boys! Let's throw out the first pitch.

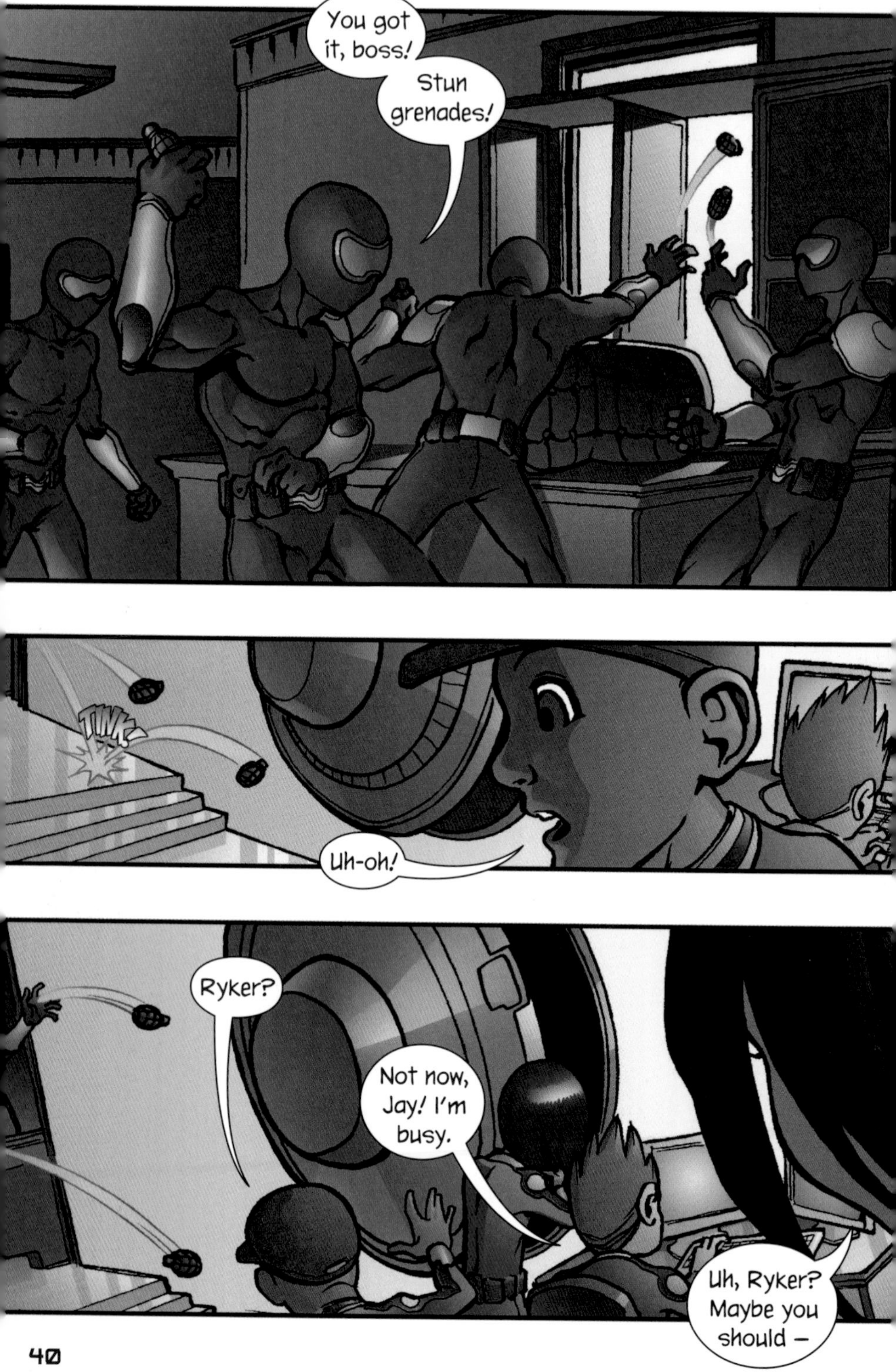
You got it, boss!
Stun grenades!
TINK!
Uh-oh!
Ryker?
Not now, Jay! I'm busy.
Uh, Ryker? Maybe you should –

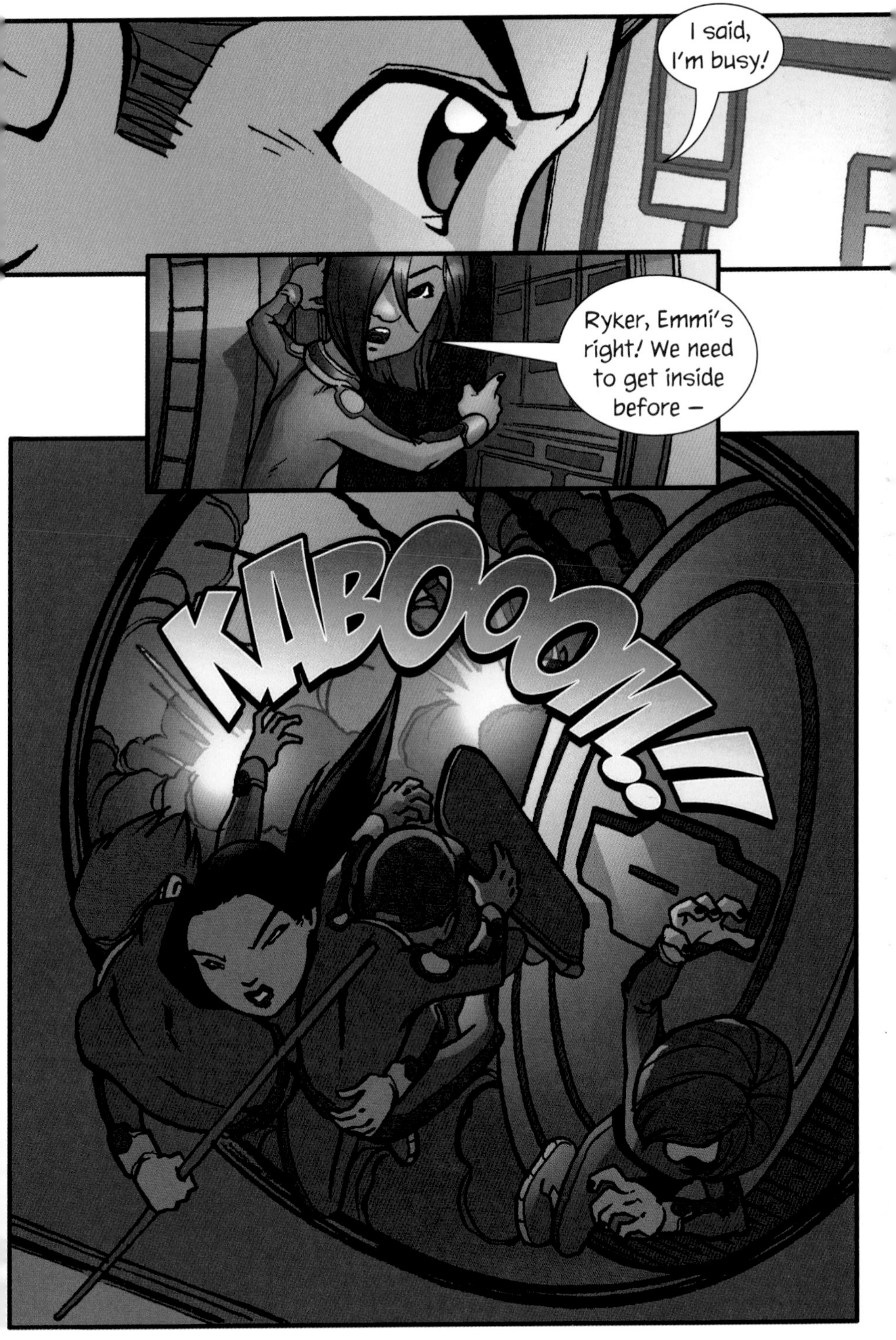
I said, I'm busy!
Ryker, Emmi's right! We need to get inside before –
KABOOOM!!!

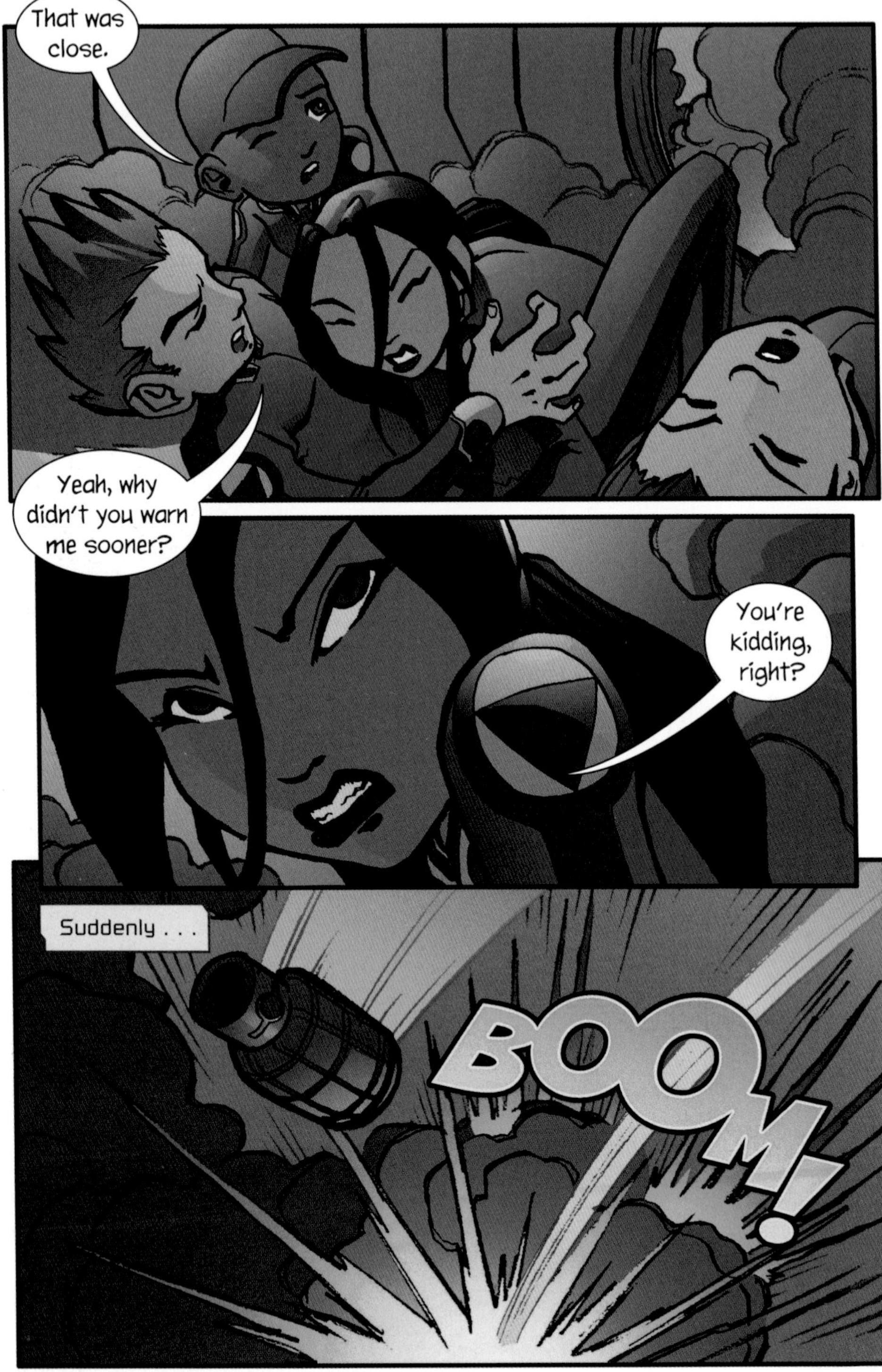
That was close.
Yeah, why didn't you warn me sooner?
You're kidding, right?
Suddenly . . .
BOOM!

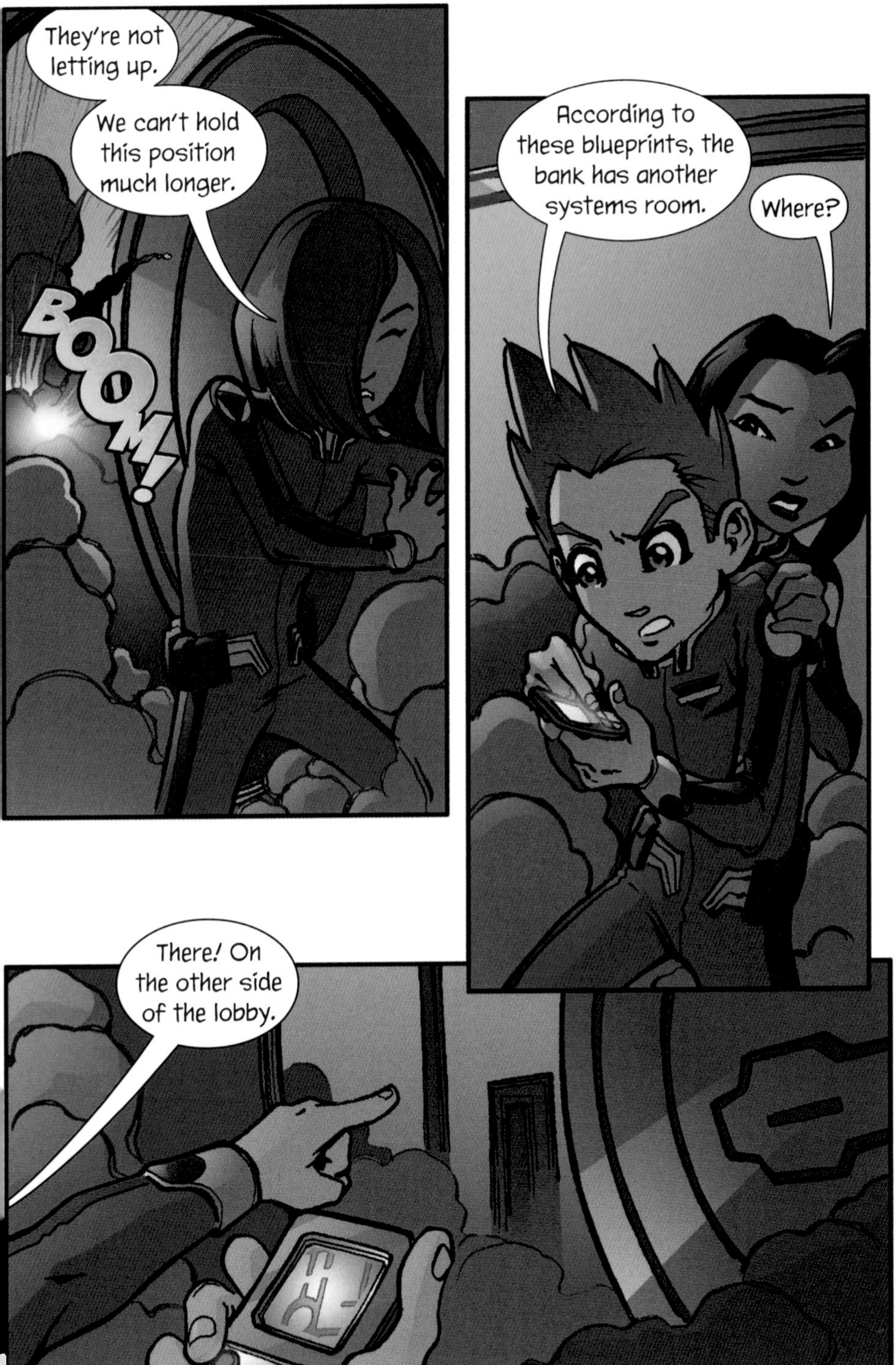
They're not letting up.
We can't hold this position much longer.
BOOM!
According to these blueprints, the bank has another systems room.
Where?
There! On the other side of the lobby.

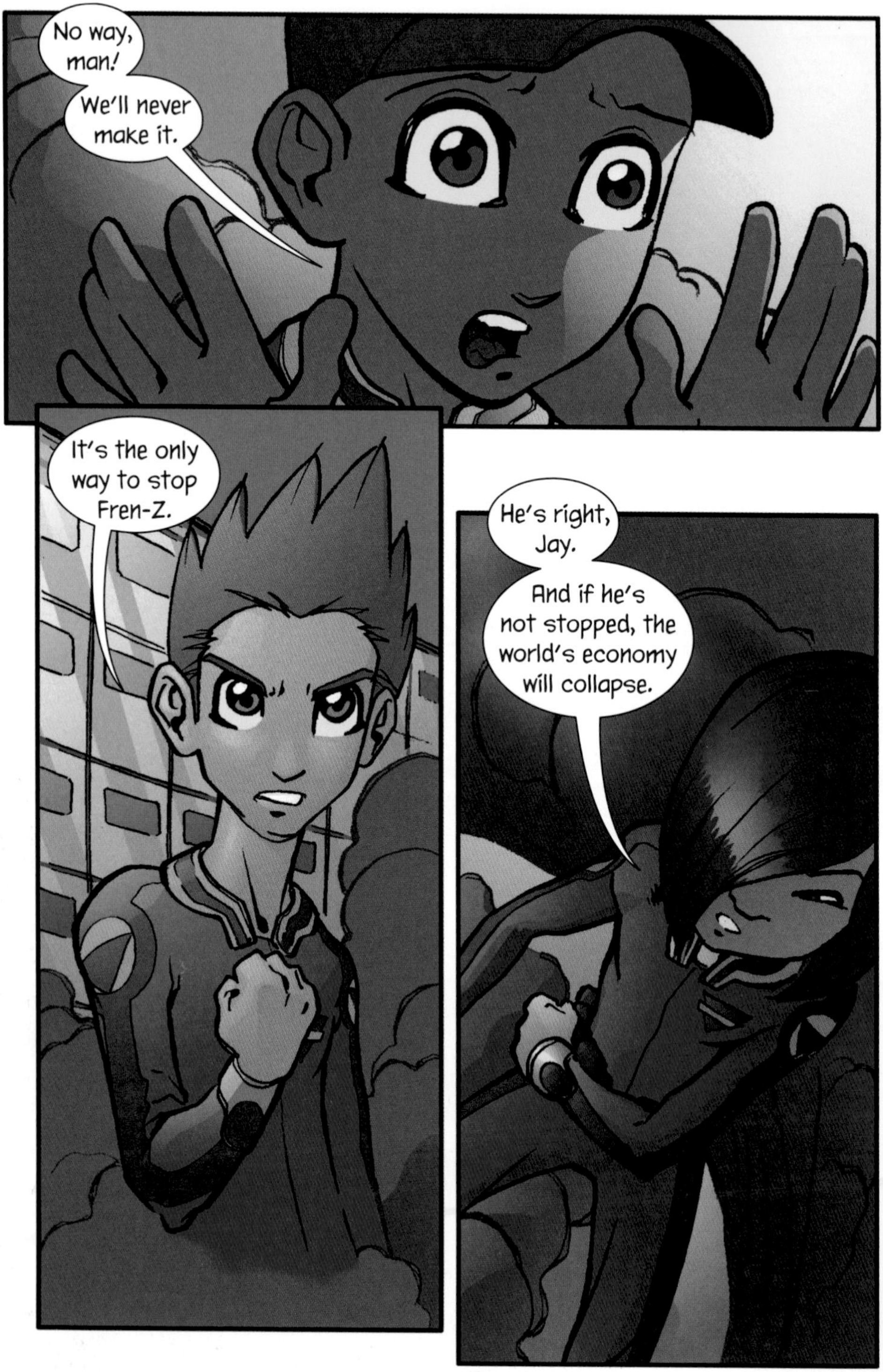
No way, man!
We'll never make it.
It's the only way to stop Fren-Z.
He's right, Jay.
And if he's not stopped, the world's economy will collapse.

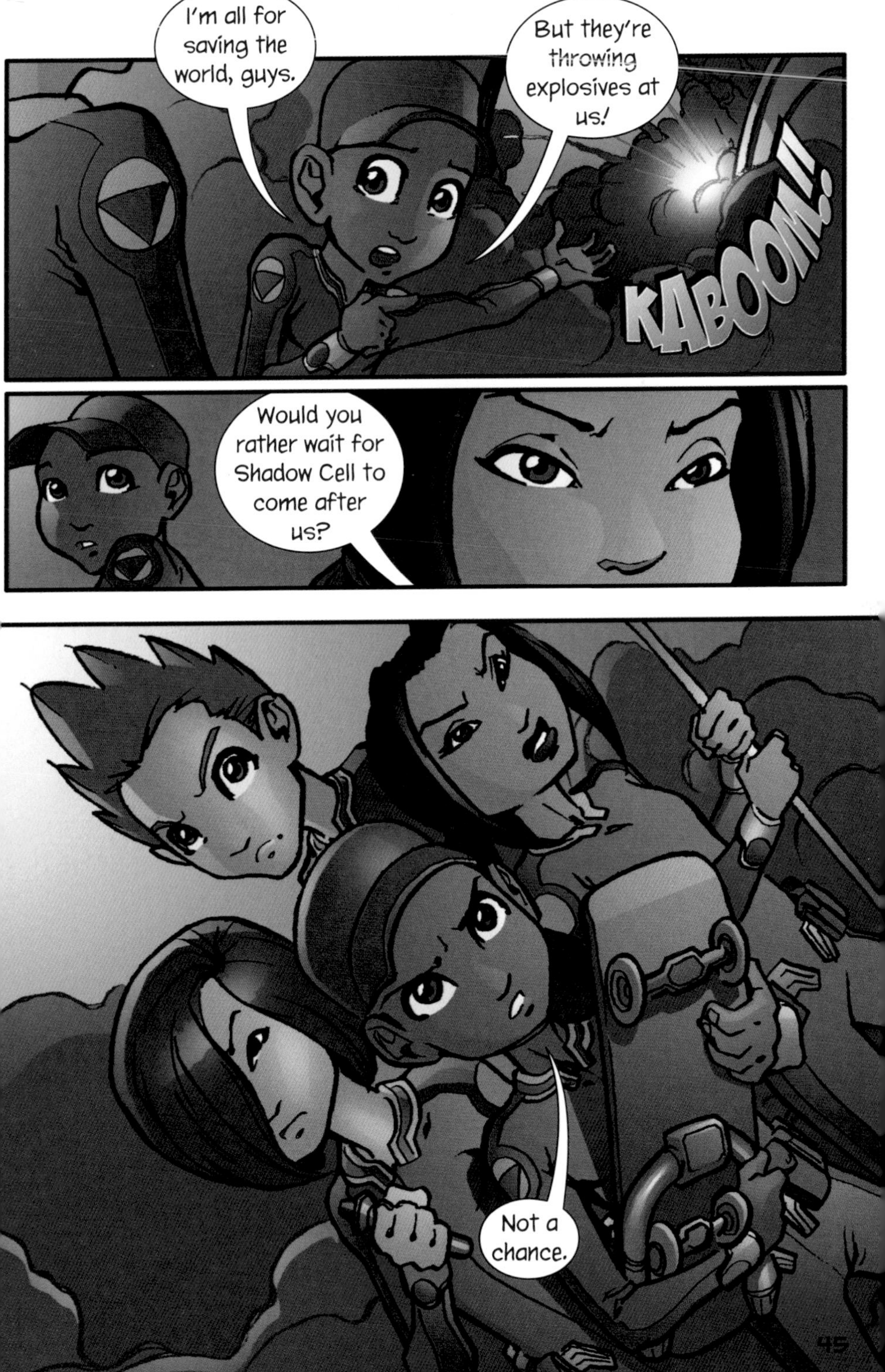
I'm all for saving the world, guys.
But they're throwing explosives at us!
KABOOM!!
Would you rather wait for Shadow Cell to come after us?
Not a chance.

SECTION

6

ACCESS GRANTED ▶▶▶▶

RYKER
COMPUTERS

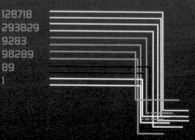

128718
293829
9283
98289
89
1

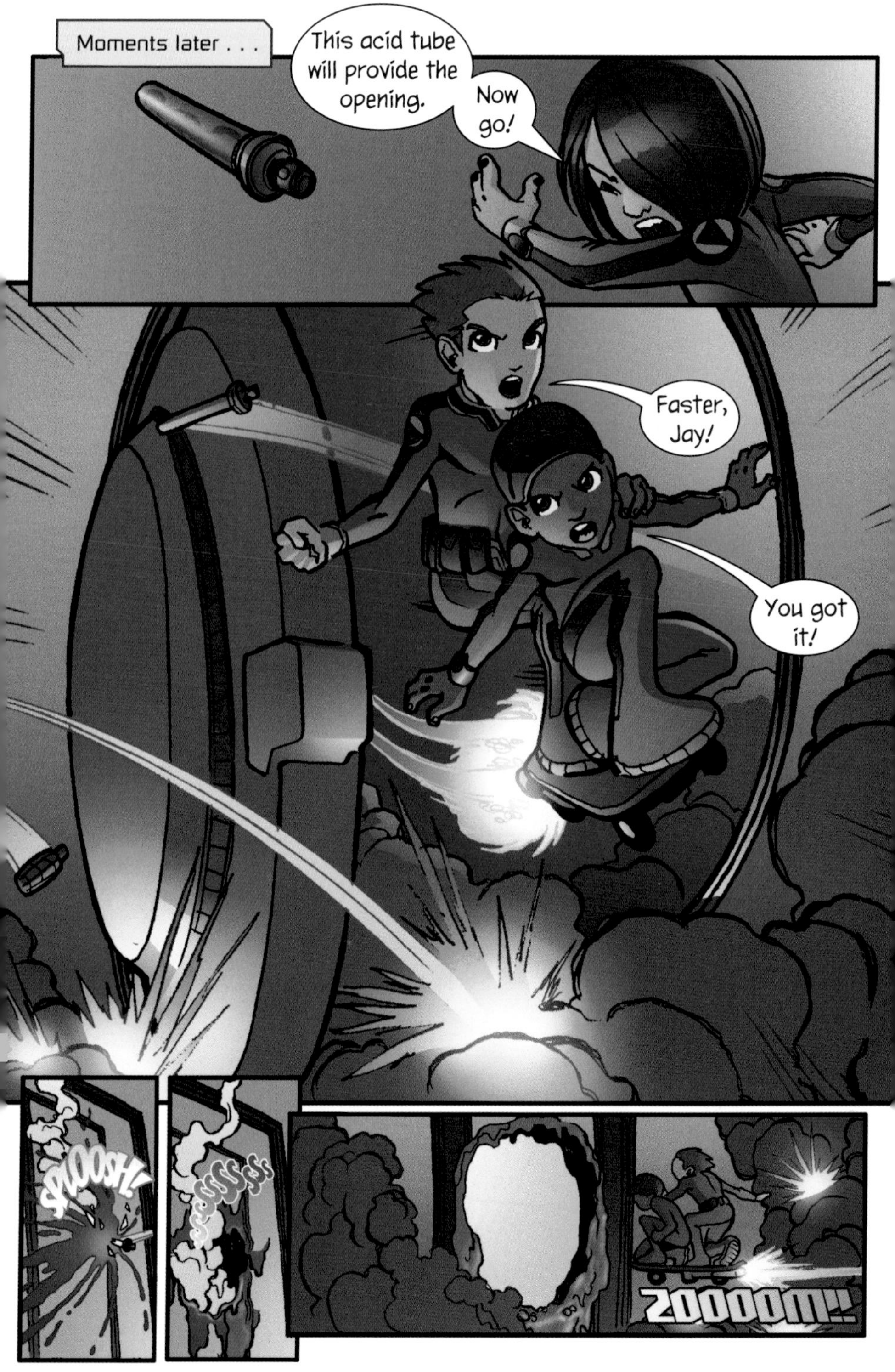
Moments later . . .
This acid tube will provide the opening.
Now go!
Faster, Jay!
You got it!
SPLOOSH!
SSSSSSSSS
ZOOOOOM!!

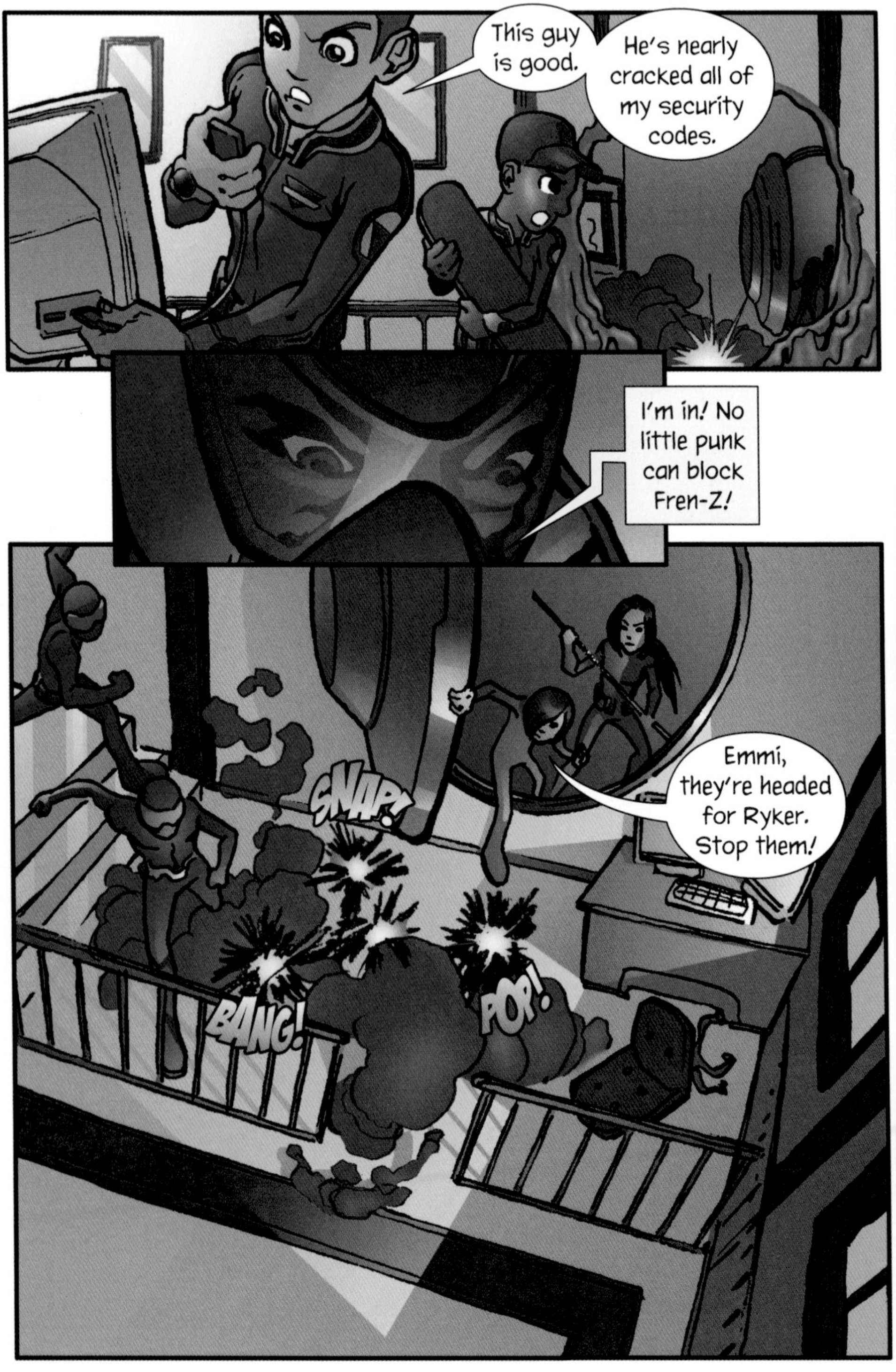
This guy is good.
He's nearly cracked all of my security codes.
I'm in! No little punk can block Fren-Z!
Emmi, they're headed for Ryker. Stop them!
SNAP!
BANG!
POP!

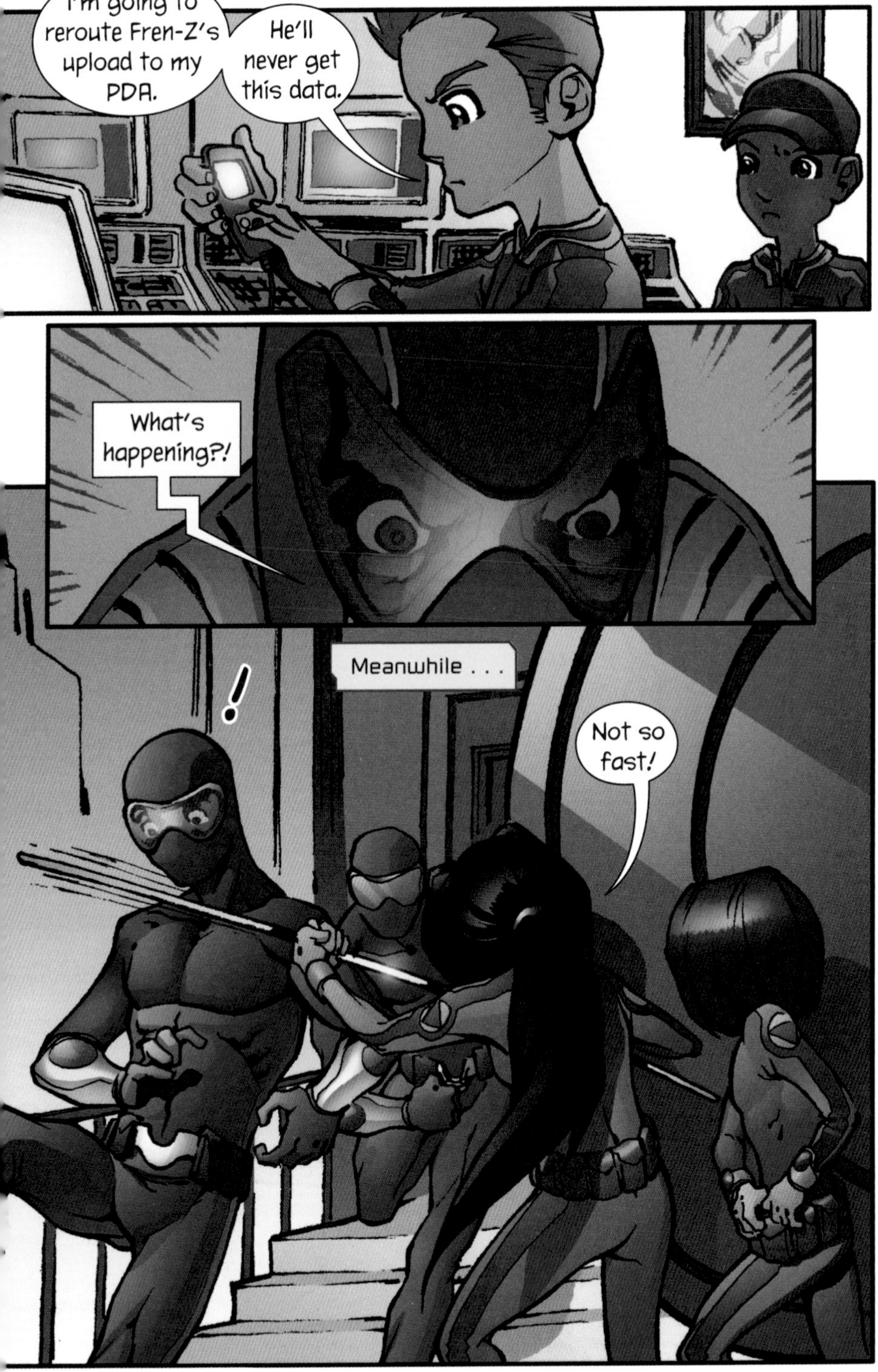
I'm going to reroute Fren-Z's upload to my PDA.
He'll never get this data.
What's happening?!
Meanwhile . . .
!
Not so fast!

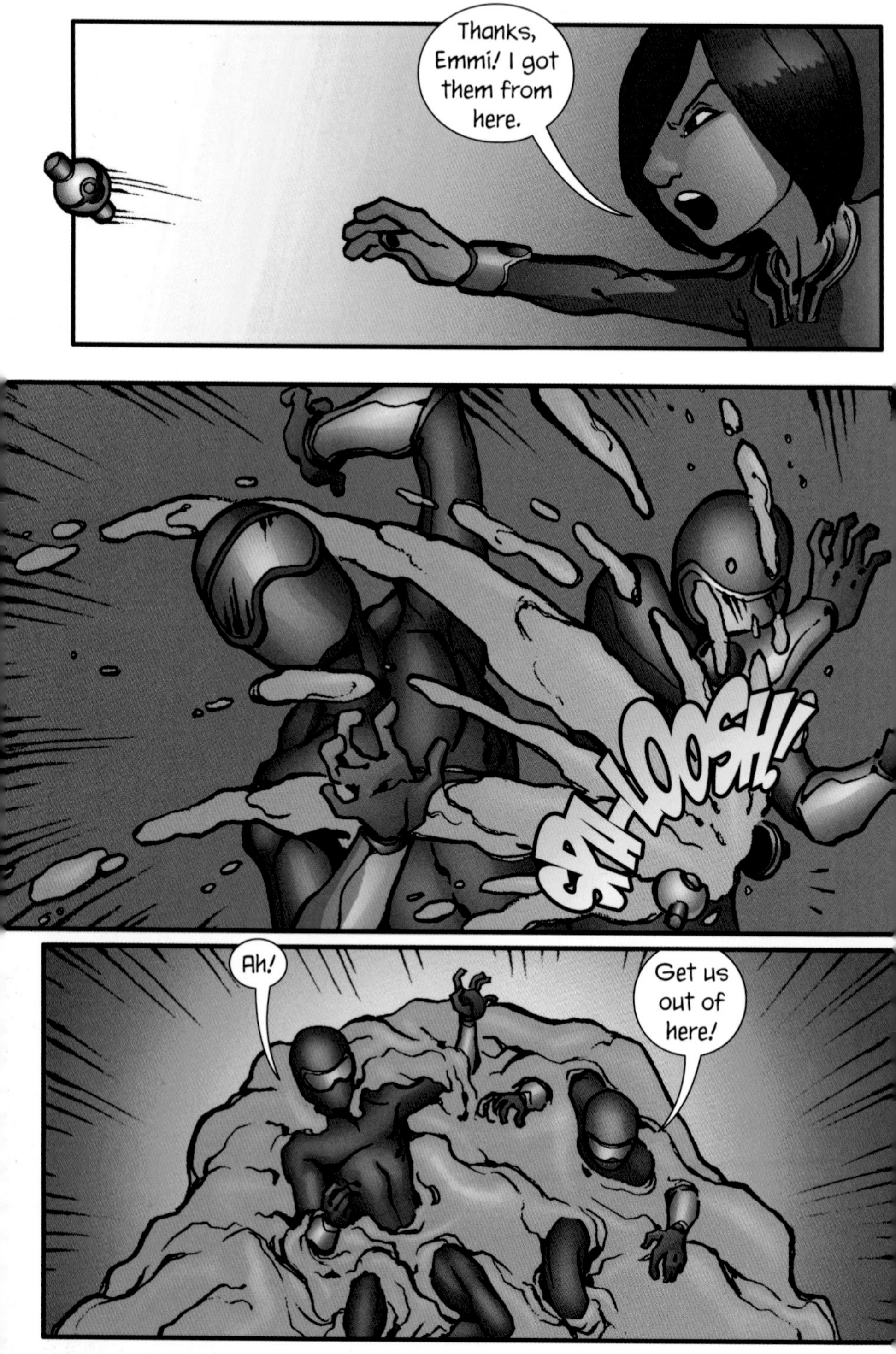
Thanks, Emmi! I got them from here.
SPLOOSH!
Ah!
Get us out of here!

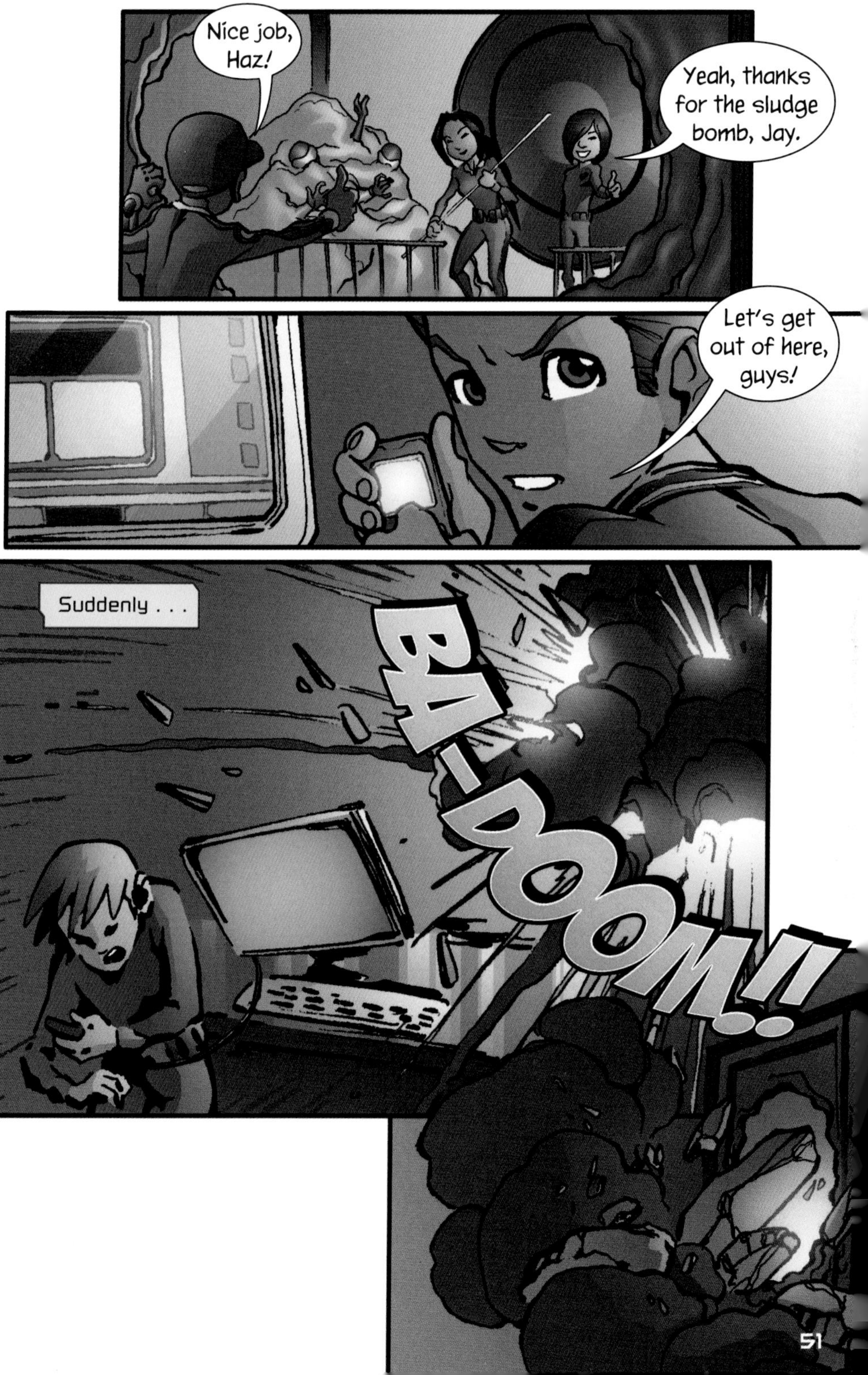
Nice job, Haz!
Yeah, thanks for the sludge bomb, Jay.
Let's get out of here, guys!
Suddenly . . .
BA-DOOM!!

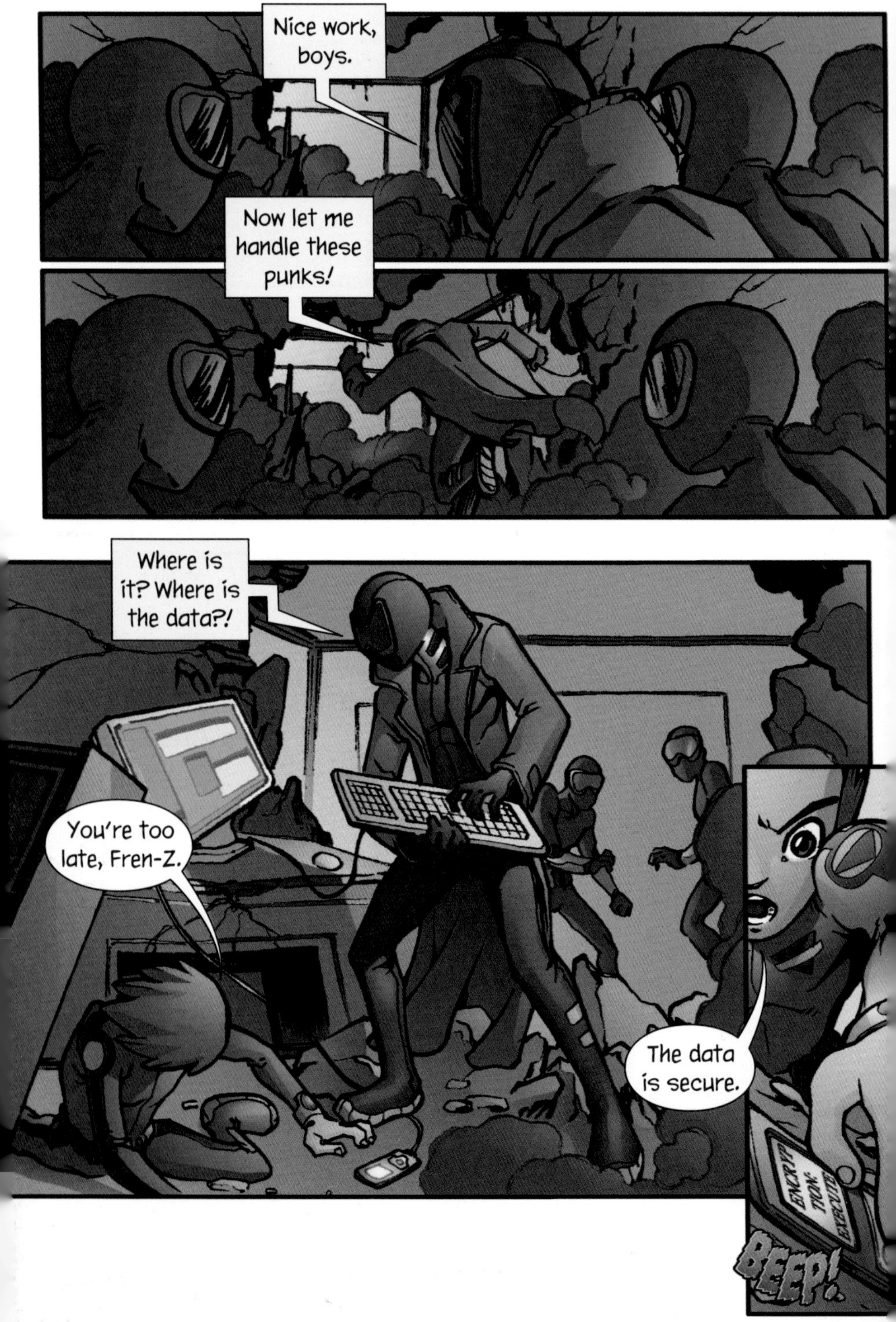

Nice work, boys.
Now let me handle these punks!
Where is it? Where is the data?!
You're too late, Fren-Z.
The data is secure.
ENCRYPTION: EXECUTED
BEEP!

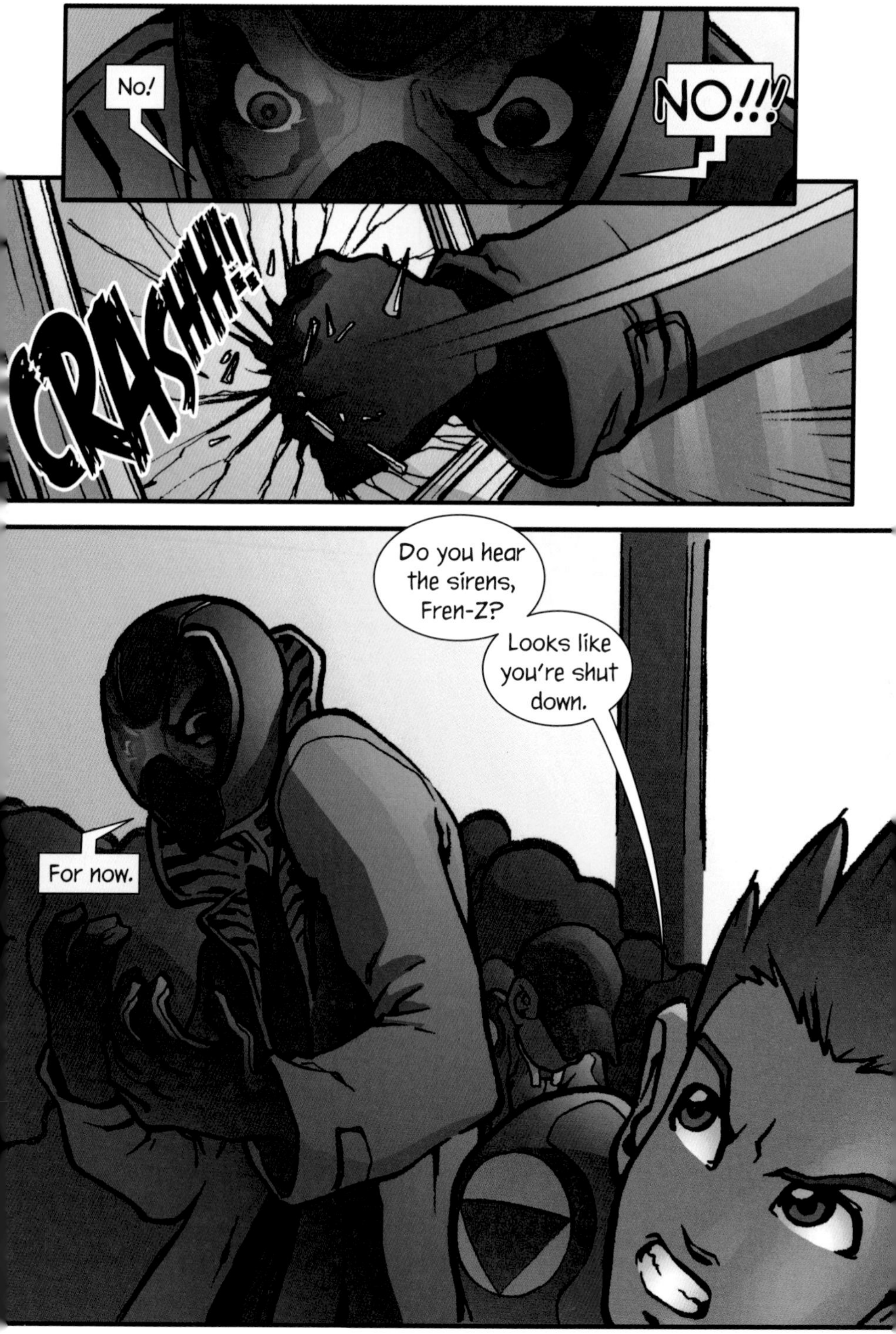
No!
NO!!!
CRASHH!!
Do you hear the sirens, Fren-Z?
Looks like you're shut down.
For now.

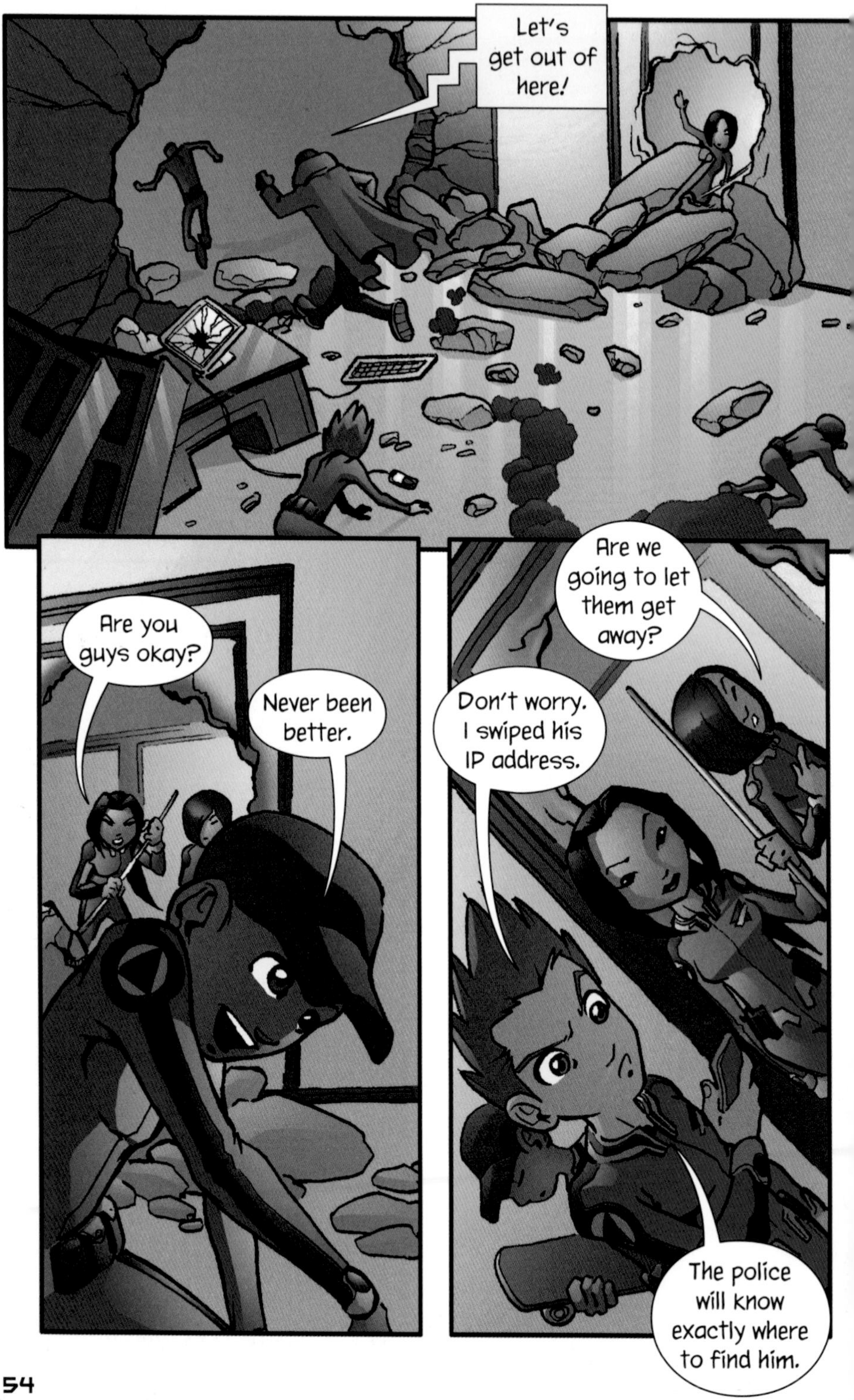
Let's get out of here!
Are you guys okay?
Never been better.
Are we going to let them get away?
Don't worry. I swiped his IP address.
The police will know exactly where to find him.

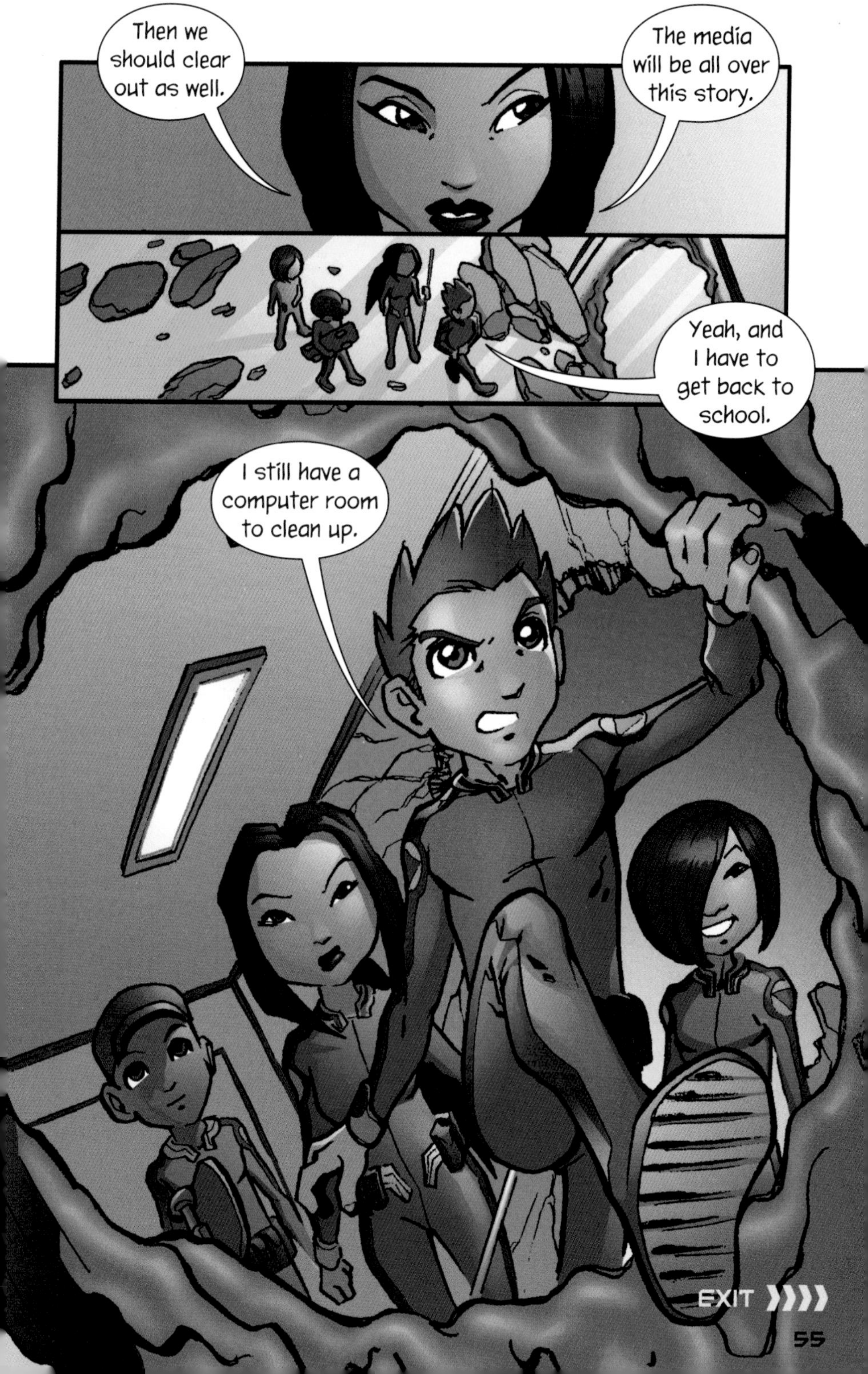
Then we should clear out as well.
The media will be all over this story.
Yeah, and I have to get back to school.
I still have a computer room to clean up.
EXIT

SPYSPACE

a place for international spies

PROFILE

NAME: William Ryker

CODE NAME: Ryker

AGE: 15

HEIGHT: 5' 7"

WEIGHT: 132 lbs.

EYES: Green

HAIR: Brown

SPY ORG: Recon Academy

SPECIAL ABILITIES: Technology expert, specializing in computers and communication devices

FAVORITES: My fully-loaded flash drive and goggles capable of computer monitoring

QUOTE: "Be nice to nerds. Chances are you'll end up working for one." –Bill Gates

PHOTOS

HOME SEARCH BROWSE LOGOUT

FRIENDS

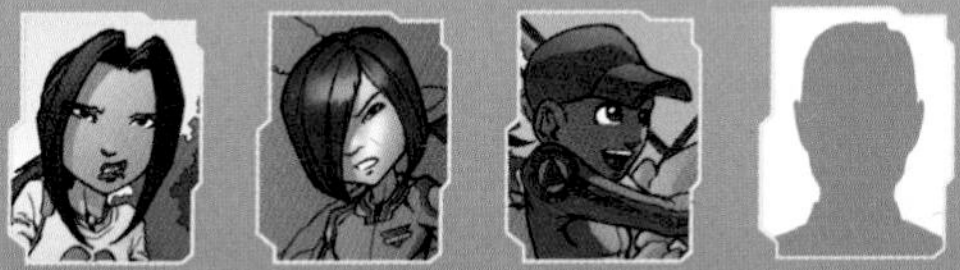

Emmi Haz Jay 007

BLOG

recent posts see all

Haven't posted in a while. Been busy putting the smackdown on Shadow Cell. I'm sure they'll be back, but at least that no-talent hacker Fren-Z will be unplugged for 25 to life. Let's just hope he doesn't get net access in the big house ;) Anyway, thanks to me, the world is safe for now. btw, check out my new pics.

Thanks to you? We never would have gotten past those goons without my hologram dogs. Nice pics, though.

Whatevs. You should be thanking me and my bo staff. It saved all of you guys :)

Keep dreaming, Em. We all know who the real hero is...btw, Ryker, how'd the cleanup go? Did anyone notice you blew up the comp room?

:o Oops! I totally forgot. Gotta go.

⟩ CASE FILE

CASE: "The Hidden Face of Fren-Z"
CASE NUMBER: 9781434211651
AGENT: Ryker
ORGANIZATION: Recon Academy

SUSPECT: Fren-Z

OVERVIEW: As the newest
member of the Shadow Cell gang,
Fren-Z has quickly made a name
for himself as the world's most
notorious hacker

CRIMINAL RECORD:
- Fraud
- Data transfer theft
- Software piracy
- Cyber terrorism
- Hacking
- Cyber stalking

INTELLIGENCE:

hacker (HA-kuhr)—a person who illegally gains access
and tampers with info in a computer system; also known
as cracker or system intruder.

computer virus (kuhm-PYOO-tur VYE-ruhss)—a computer
program designed to damage or destroy information

worm (WURM)—a computer program that attacks and
damages computers

HISTORY:

Hackers have been around since computers were invented. During the 1960s, students at the Massachusetts Institute of Technology became some of the first hackers. They created programming shortcuts for the school's new mainframe computer.

In the 1970s, phone hackers called "phreaks" used their skills to commit crimes. They built small devices called blue boxes, which allowed them to make free phone calls. Two of these phreaks were Steve Wozniak and Steve Jobs, the founders of Apple Computers.

By the 1980s, more hackers were committing crimes. In 1986, the U.S. Congress passed the Computer Fraud and Abuse Act. This law made it illegal to access a computer system without permission.

The law has not stopped hackers. In 2000, one hacker released a virus called Love Bug. When users opened an "ILOVEYOU" e-mail, their computers were infected. Love Bug caused more damage than any other virus.

CONCLUSION:

Although technology will protect future computers, only the Recon Academy can truly secure cyberspace.

› ABOUT THE AUTHOR

Chris Everheart always dreamed of interesting places, fascinating people, and exciting adventures. He is still a dreamer. He enjoys writing thrilling stories about young heroes who live in a world that doesn't always understand them. Chris lives in Minneapolis, Minnesota, with his family. He plans to travel to every continent on the globe, see interesting places, meet fascinating people, and have exciting adventures.

› ABOUT THE ILLUSTRATOR

Arcana Studios, Inc. was founded by Sean O'Reilly in Coquitlam, British Columbia, in 2004. Four years later, Arcana has established itself as Canada's largest comic book and graphic novel publisher with over 100 comics and 9 books released. A nomination for a Harvey Award and winning the "Schuster Award for Top Publisher" are just a few of Arcana's accolades. The studio is known as a quality publisher for independent comic books and graphic novels.

) GLOSSARY

firewall (FIRE-wawl)—collection of electronic security measures that prevents access to a computer network

IP address (EYE PEE uh-DRESS)—Internet Protocol address; the number assigned to each computer connected to the Internet

motherboard (MUHTH-er-bohrd)—board that contains the basic circuitry of a computer

overloaded (oh-vur-LODE-id)—sent too much electricity through a circuit, causing a burnout

platoon (pluh-TOON)—a group of soldiers made up of two or more squads

prototype (PROH-toh-tipe)—the first version of an invention that tests an idea to see if it will work

terminal (TUR-muh-nul)—a device used to enter information into a computer

) DISCUSSION QUESTIONS

1. Ryker's computer skills helped take down the hacker Fren-Z. Do you think Ryker could have solved the case without help from the other Recon Academy members? Why or why not?

2. Each member of the Recon Academy is different. Which character is most like you? Explain your answer.

3. Each page of a graphic novel has several illustrations called panels. What is your favorite panel in this book? Describe what you like about the illustration and why it's your favorite.

1. Each member of the Recon Academy has a unique talent. Describe your own skill or talent.

2. At the end of the story, the Recon Academy helps capture Fren-Z, but other members of the Shadow Cell are still on the loose. Write a story about what will happen next. Will Shadow Cell strike again?

3. Many comic books are written and illustrated by two different people. Write a story, and then give it to a friend to illustrate.